After the Funeral

After the Funeral

Al McLachlan

Ekstasis Editions

AN EKSTASIS NOIR BOOK

Library and Archives Canada Cataloguing in Publication

MacLachlan, Al

    After the funeral / Al MacLachlan.

ISBN 1-894800-78-8

    I. Title.

PS8625.L327A72 2006   C813'.6   C2006-906619-9

Acknowledgement:
Thank you to Stuart Young for his valuable assistance proofing, and help editing
After the Funeral .

Published in 2006 by:
Ekstasis Editions Canada Ltd.   Ekstasis Editions
Box 8474, Main Postal Outlet   Box 571
Victoria, B.C. V8W 3S1   Banff, Alberta T0L 0C0

THE CANADA COUNCIL | LE CONSEIL DES ARTS
FOR THE ARTS | DU CANADA
SINCE 1957 | DEPUIS 1957

BRITISH
COLUMBIA
ARTS COUNCIL
Supported by the Province of British Columbia

After the Funeral has been published with the assistance of grants from the Canada Council for the Arts and the British Columbia Arts Council administered by the Cultural Services Branch of British Columbia.

*This book is dedicated with love to
Victor, Lynn and Leila.*

After the Funeral

All I know is that there is suffering and that there are none guilty; that cause follows effect, simply and directly; that everything flows and finds its level.

Dostoevsky

Prologue

Vito and Frank had watched Rory Jesson leave for work. They were sitting in a white van, which had an official looking logo on the doors. They were both wearing security guard uniforms Vito had picked up through a contact of Fillipone's. Frank had complained, but Vito told him that for what they were going do, they should look official.

"Just what are we gonna do, Vito?" Frank asked unpleasantly.

"We're gonna case the joint. Pull a B&E. He may have sent some stuff from New York up here, Tony said. So..."

"So?" Frank looked at him in anticipation.

"So we do what Tony wants, what d'you think?" Vito looked over at Frank who was watching a tall woman waltz out of the condo next to Jesson's.

"Hey, catch that action, Vito."

Vito followed his gaze, and without missing a beat said, "That's a guy. What are you? Turning gearbox on me."

"No way." Frank went beet red, as he clued in. "Fuck, Vito. I could never do that."

"Do what?" Vito replied, hoping to aggravate Frank some more.

"Dress up as a bitch. Imagine what the guys would think!"

"Come to think about it, no." Vito snorted. Frank was still staring at the whatever-the-fuck it was.

"Yeow! How can they do that?"

"Do what?"

"Have their cocks cut off."

"They don't have them cut off, Frank. The cocks are inverted. Don't you know nothing?"

"No way!" But Frank wasn't so sure now. He watched the trannie disappear. "Shit. That'd be vicious when they get a hard on."

Vito rolled his eyes.

"Hey, c'mon, let's go." Vito grabbed a satchel, handed a larger empty bag to Frank. They got out of the car and ambled over to the entrance. Vito motioned for Frank to stop and offered him a cigarette. Frank took the smoke and lit it.

"What're we doing, Vito?"

"We're taking a smoke break, and waiting for someone to come out that door." He moved his shoulder to indicate the direction of the door behind them.

"Why can't we do this at night, when there's no one around?" Frank asked as he dragged on his smoke, flicking the ash on the pavement.

"Because he's probably home at night. You know Frank," Vito said turning to look him in the eyes. "Tony's right, you're a lot more intelligent when you keep your fucking mouth zipped." Vito looked past Frank at the door to the complex.

"I thought we were buddies, Vito."

"We are Frank, we are ... Okay. Someone's coming out. Put out your smoke and head for the door. Let me do the talking."

The two walked towards the door as a middle aged lady was coming out.

"Nice day, lady." Vito said with a big smile. "Thanks," he said again as she smiled back holding the door open for them.

Inside, Susanne was walking around the apartment in a sheer silk negligee. She stopped at the computer and noticed that the screen had a message to Rory from Pete Fraser. She was about to check the e-mail when she heard a noise, and looked around towards the door. In the living room two men were standing quietly. They hadn't expected her to be here. And obviously Susanne didn't expect them. She froze.

"Who are you? What are you doing here?" She asked bravely after a seemingly long silence. She hoped they didn't hear the fear she felt in her voice.

"We're security. The neighbours phoned. The door was open." Vito said blankly.

"No it wasn't ... Oh, I guess my boyfriend left it ajar. Anyway there's no problem. Can I see some ID?" Susanne asked suspiciously, and walked toward Vito.

"Sure." Vito reached into his pocket and pulled out a gun. He aimed it at her head, which was now only five feet away. Frank maneuvered behind Susanne.

"Be very quite." Vito said softly. "And you won't get hurt." Susanne immediately jumped back almost into Frank's arms, who reached out and grabbed her.

"We're gonna have to kill her, you realize?" Frank said to Vito. Susanne started to scream, but Frank put his big hand over her mouth.

"Why?" For a change Vito was not thinking very clearly.

"She saw us Vito, whadda you think?" Vito was still staring at Susanne's body. Susanne's eyes were in a complete panic.

"Yeah, now she also knows my name you goof. But yeah. Fuck, what a waste. She's fucking beautiful." Susanne, regaining some bit of inner strength, bit Frank's hand as hard as she could. Frank instinctively yelled out, "You little bitch!" and at the same time brought his other hand with the gun down on the side of her head. Blood spurted out, covering the gun and Frank's hand. Now both his hands were bloody.

"Fuck, she peed all over me." Frank wiped his hands on his coveralls, and kind of pulled the part she'd peed on away from his leg. "Hey, let's find what we're looking for, and get the fuck out of here."

Vito checked the body for a pulse, then took charge again. "She's dead. Collect any files, tapes, computer disks — the same as last time — and put them in that bag I gave you."

The two men went through the study, the living room and the rest of the two bedroom condo. They poured documents, files and computer disks into the bags. Vito looked at the computer, saw the e-mail, read it, then inserted a CD disk into the computer.

"What's that fucking for?" Frank asked, wiping his pants with a cloth.

"It'll erase the hard drive. We can't take the computer with us, right? Let's get going."

"What do we do about her?"

"What can we do? She's dead." Vito said, getting pissed off with Frank's inane questions.

"We can make it look like the kid did it." Frank said complacently.

Vito thought about this for a second or two. "You're right. Another B&E would look suspicious. This way it puts the heat on Jesson. Tony'll be happy about this." He looked around the living room, "What you do is put on a glove and whack her in the nose. She falls on her head right here." Vito pointed to the fireplace where the brick stood out sharply. "Covering the place on her head where you whapped her. It's simple."

Vito held the body up and Frank did as he was told punching her right on the nose. Vito let her fall almost exactly where he planned onto the edge of the brick. "It's not perfect, but it'll keep the cops guessing for awhile," Vito said as they crossed to the door. "Leave the door open a bit, the cops'll get here quicker."

Chapter One

Rory woke up in Victory Square, Vancouver. It is a tiny square in the centre of the old downtown where the war memorial stands, but for decades it had been taken over by pigeons and the homeless. Rory found himself surrounded by tramps. And he had an enormous hangover. His body was in such agony that he could hardly move. The pain seemed to emanate from his rectum. He realized he was still half-pissed and he wondered what he could have done to feel so bad. Had he been rolled? That was what he finally figured had happened. As he sat up, an older man — he could've been forty or seventy — in a soiled dark jacket and mismatched working pants that were covered in mud stains, approached him.

"Hey, got a smoke, buddy?"

Rory looked at him not sure if he did or not. Do I smoke? he thought. I should know. He laughed as he searched his pockets.

"No, I guess I don't smoke."

"You guess you don't? You'd think you'd remember. I never seen you here before ... what's your name?"

"Rory?" Again he paused, his mind was terribly confused. He didn't seem to remember anything about himself. Is it Rory?

That's an odd name. What do I do? "I think." he added, trying to be sincere.

"Roy, you think. Whatever you were drinking last night, man, I want some. The name's Jake. Jake the Rake, they used to call me."

"I can't remember much of anything. I must've got rolled."

"You gotta watch it around here. They killed Andy a few weeks back. Kicked him to death. Maybe he never knew. He was usually pretty pissed. I like to think that anyway." When Rory looked at him his eyes were so sad that Jake was taken back. "You going to the shelter?" Jake asked, to change the subject.

"Where's that?"

"C'mon, I'll take you, get some food and coffee into ya. Maybe you'll remember what the fuck you had to drink last night."

Rory looked confused, but followed Jake to a line-up on Cordova Street outside a church mission. He waited in line for some time, then when Jake started talking to someone he knew, Rory wandered off like some sort of zombie.

Rory walked the streets of the east-end apparently looking for his home. He knew he needed to find something, but was not sure what that was. He started to recognize some things. First it was familiar roads signs, then buildings he'd seen before. He stopped at Oppenheimer Park and asked two strangers if they knew him. They looked at him figuring he was on drugs, scratched their heads, laughed at each other, and took off. Rory continued walking, then as if a ray of sunshine reflected off one of the dingy windows had penetrated his consciousness, his mind lit up.

"Do I have any identification on me?" he asked out loud, slapping his pants as he did so. A Chinese woman carrying some groceries looked up startled, watching him pulling out his pockets. Rory looked at them to find what he figured he'd find, nothing. The lady shook her head and carried on. But in his jacket, although it seemed too big to be his jacket, there was a wallet. It contained no ID, only five twenty-dollar bills. As if struck by some sign from god the poor slob realized he was starving. Like an android summoned, he headed into a café to wolf down steak and eggs with hash browns and a side of pancakes. All the while drinking coffee like it was going out of style.

When he'd finished Rory sat idle for some time feeling satisfied, but then he abruptly got up, paid the waitress and went back on the street. He walked for hours in an ambivalent direction, recognizing some signs, but feeling like he was in a foreign place. Am I even from here? The thought struck making him wobble. He stopped and asked directions off a man in a blue delivery uniform who told him that he was going in the wrong direction for the city centre. Downtown was the other way. And in fact, he was almost in Burnaby.

"You from outta town?" asked the man.

"No," answered Rory not really sure. Then added, "I think I must've been hit on the head, 'cause my memory's ..." he hesitated, waiting for the right word, "not working how it was." The man pointed to Exhibition Park across the street.

"That's the PNE. Remember that? Maybe you used to go there as a teenager?" The man figured Rory must have been rolled and was sympathetic.

Rory vaguely remembered it, but not from his teens. "Are there horse races there?" he asked, remembering a sunny afternoon.

"You bet," the man said smiling. Rory hadn't heard that expression for some time, but he got the pun after a little thought, and managed to crack a smile back at the man. He thanked the man and headed across the street. He took the guy's advice and caught a bus down to a place he instantly recognized — the Smilin' Buddha sign at Hastings and Carrall. He stepped down onto a sidewalk that was covered with litter, cigarette butts and stains which could have been blood, urine or compressed shit, walked up to the door. It was closed and looked like it had been for sometime. Vivid images of a punk rock concert filled his head. Some punk in black leaping off the stage and attacking someone who was spewing beer at him. The whole room burst into a scene from a bad western. But it was all fake ... Now Rory remembered. It was a concert he had video-taped. Was he a cameraman? It didn't sound right. He thought of himself as someone who had a pretty quiet job, maybe in an office?

Now at least he knew where he was and he walked down towards the pawnshops, which were also familiar. He was fascinated by the old cameras in the second-hand shops and asked each of the countermen if they'd recalled seeing him in the store before. Most of them shook their heads, or grunted in the negative, few of them were talkative types. After an hour of this he walked into a tavern, the old style type that still had doors for Ladies & Escorts, and ordered a beer.

By the time he came out the sun had gone down and it was getting dark. Rory was surprised. He'd only had two beer, where had the time gone? And he noticed that he wasn't walking as steadily as he had been, and people were out of focus until just before he almost walked into them.

What had happened was that Rory had passed out during his second beer, and because this was a common occurrence at this particular establishment, and it wasn't very busy anyway, and perhaps because Rory had given large tips, the waiters had let him have a little nap. And it wasn't just the beer that was affecting Rory's balance and vision, the drugs he'd taken over the past two weeks combined with the alcohol were mixing up inside him like some Molotov cocktail.

As he tried to focus to find some direction, feeling very much like a homeless drunk, which to all intents and purposes he was, he felt himself drifting into some dream. When he next was able to grasp anything consciously he was on a dingy looking street watching a panhandler play guitar outside what used to be a government liquor store. He vaguely recognized the song, and when the guy had finished and Rory had clapped enthusiastically he asked what the song was.

"Whiskey and Wimmen," replied the musician. "John Lee Hooker."

"I've heard it before," Rory said. "But years ago it seems."

"That'd be about right. It's old."

"Well thanks," said Rory and dropped a couple of loonies into the guy's battered guitar case. Then remembering the Smilin' Buddha, he asked if there were any TV stations close by. The guy thought for a moment.

"There's one somewhere on the other side of the Cambie bridge, I believe. They videotaped me awhile ago. Never did see it though." He gave the basic directions to Rory who thanked him and moved on. It was getting cold and he drew his jacket around him. He wasn't tired but he was wondering where he could sleep tonight. He almost went back and asked the musician, but decided that if he could find the TV station, someone there might recognize him.

Only he never got there. As he turned the corner and found himself in an alley he was again overcome with hallucinations and a feeling of acute paranoia.

Rory stumbled down the alley. He saw a familiar looking woman (Roxanne, though he didn't know her name) standing in the back entrance way to an old and shabby Chinese restaurant. The door was green and above it was a hand-painted sign, The Green Door. Rory felt he was in some film from the 1930s. It was both familiar and frightening. He expected some Chinese gangster to come out wielding a machete, and he cowered back on the other side of the alley.

Roxanne beckoned him like a hooker. As he started to approach she brazenly and seductively strode down the alley, then, like an apparition, disappeared into another doorway. Rory rubbed his eyes because everything kept going out of focus, but he followed hypnotically, for he realized that she was an important clue, a recent memory, someone who might help him remember who he was. When he got to the doorway though, he was completely appalled by what he saw. Inside the open door was a tiny, filthy room, with a cheap bed and some ratty yellow curtains behind it. The woman had shockingly changed from being the assertive seductress he'd seen into a mousy, nervous and apparently hopeless junkie. She was sitting on the edge of the bed with a syringe in her right hand. All her concentration was fixed on sticking the murky liquid within into the throbbing vein of her other arm. Rory saw the liquid mix with blood and watched fascinated as she loosened a piece of elastic around her biceps then hammered the lever down. She lay back for some time obviously in rapture, then looked up at Rory with dazed eyes. She smiled and stupidly offered the empty syringe to Rory, who was repulsed and staggered back, falling onto a chair.

He became aware of a thick fog floating in the room and his eyes were hazy. When the fog cleared he found that the room was now a prison cell and everything from a moment ago had disappeared as if in a dream. He could see the woman getting up and as she came towards him Rory saw that it was not a woman, but a man dressed in leather like some sadomasochist.

In his hand was not the needle Rory had seen earlier but a long stiletto knife. And the face of the man, which Rory saw as intrinsically evil, was a face he knew, and he trembled, feeling the horror of being fixated to the chair. (In fact, it was the face of Henning.)

"Tell me where the tapes are Rory," he said, his eyeballs so close Rory could see all the veins, giving him an insane look which made Rory freeze in his chair. But just as quickly as Henning had appeared, he vanished and Rory was left looking at a figure lying in a contorted shape on the bed.

It took him some time to unglue himself from the chair. And when he had done so he cautiously approached the bed. The moment he could see the body clearly he immediately stopped. It appeared to be dead. Rory tried to remember whether he had ever seen a dead body and then was horrifyingly aware that he'd had seen this one before. Her face was covered in blood and what appeared to be dark bruises. Her blond hair was streaked with dark red congealed blood. Her arms were at impossibly grotesque angles and Rory assumed one or both had been broken. "Suzanne," he said aloud. "It's Suzanne." The memory came so violently tears burst from his eyes. He sat down on the bed and wept.

After some time he looked back at the body, but it was gone. Rory rose, not sure if he was in a dream or had taken psychedelic drugs. As he left the room he looked back at the bed as if to be sure that his mind wasn't playing tricks on him, but the body was still gone. All that remained was a single bed, covered in a ratty Salvation Army blanket.

Although he wasn't aware of it, when he came out of the doorway he was being watched through night-vision binoculars. Approximately two hundred feet away Roxanne Mallory was sitting in a nondescript black car. She had been observing

Rory on and off for several hours, and was surprised when at one time he walked right by her without the least bit of recognition at all. Henning had told her that his memory was temporarily shot, but nonetheless it was unnerving. Her job was to make sure Rory didn't get into too much trouble, get picked up by the police, and mainly to find out where he was going. They'd placed a transponder bug in his wallet so she didn't have to follow too closely, but she had become worried and gone into the room after Rory had not come out for sometime, only to see him frozen in a chair. This time he appeared terrified of her, and she had gone back outside. She sipped a coffee as she saw him go back along the alley the way he had come in, but instead of going back onto the street he appeared to go into the back door of The Green Door.

Rory knew he had been here before, but he could not remember when. At first glance he saw poorly-dressed men eating cheap Chinese food at a counter. Then he saw himself sitting there, talking to a young Chinese girl. But this he knew was some sort of vision, because he was several years younger, and he remembered the occasion. It was his first year in Vancouver and a beautiful Korean girl had taken him to what she called a "Vancouver institution." She had told him that downstairs there was alleged to be an opium den where the Chinese and later the beatniks used to go to smoke a pipe. Remembering this, Rory went down some rickety, twisting stairs to find himself in a smoky, dimly-lit room. Some people were sitting there smoking large hookah pipes, others were passed out and contentedly lying on cots. He could smell the opium. As he breathed it in he felt dizzy and his vision went hazy again. For a long time he walked along painted corridors trying to find his way out. There were rooms attached, but he did not enter them. He followed the corridor, which was painted like some

Expressionist had gone wild, up stairs, around corners. He stopped to rest, and two joggers sped by him. He wanted to call out and ask directions but they didn't hear him. He found himself at the top of some stairs and walked down. At the bottom was the restaurant again. In a panic he turned to go back up the stairs but found himself staring at a brick wall. There was a message. It said, Dawning of a New Error, and underneath that, DOA, in black paint.

When he turned back he found himself back in an alley. There was what seemed a gang of cats staring at him, hungrily with bright yellow eyes. He staggered out onto the street not knowing where he was going, but trying to get away from the nightmares he'd just seen. Nightmares or visions? He wasn't sure. But he sure as hell remembered Suzanne and kept seeing images of her, some of them on a television screen. Was she only an actress in a movie, or TV cop show? No. He was sure he lived with her. He could see her in bed. In the hot-tub. The idea of a hot tub seemed strange.

As he was trying to find some meaning in the scattered thoughts he was getting he walked through what he thought was some sort of street carnival. Girls, mainly, although some of them looked like made-up boys, were dressed in colourful, short dresses, their nylons and high heels making them look all legs. Some of the faces seemed blue, others red, but all had their faces painted and as he walked by they seemed to come closer and make gestures at him; some laughed, other asked if he wanted "some fun," or "a party." Finally, he realized he was walking through the hooker strip, and somehow was relieved, as if the panic he had been experiencing had dissipated, and he was now safe.

In her car, Roxanne followed slowly, stopping to ask directions to stall for time and to look like a tourist. The final instance she did this, by the time she was back searching for

Rory, he had disappeared. It looked like he had gone down an alley, and Roxanne drove around the block to try to get ahead of him. Her screen, however, showed that Rory was stopped somewhere in the alley. She waited. Then Rory took off in the other direction and she maneuvered around the block, only to get stuck in traffic. Never one with a lot of patience, she became frustrated while it appeared that Rory was running, or walking very fast, because he was now several blocks away to the east.

Actually, Rory wasn't. At the time he was lying in the alley rubbing his head, and trying to get up. His wallet, however, was in the pocket of the man who had knocked him down, then had headed over to the east-end. Rory slowly got up, and although his head hurt, his vision had returned more or less to normal.

He followed some people onto the Skytrain, and spent the next two hours going back and forth above the city of Vancouver, staring out the window at the lights, recognizing vaguely the mountains and some of the areas the train went through. On the way back he noticed he was being stared at by a man in a blue uniform. Police? thought Rory. No, security. Nonetheless he had a panic attack and got off at the next stop, shaking and still being stared at by the man. As it happened he found himself not too far from where he had got on the train and he shuffled along the almost-empty streets. When he got to Pender Street, he suddenly remembered where he was and headed towards the bus station. His wallet and remaining bills were gone but he found he still had some change and a fin in his pocket, and he needed a hot coffee.

When he was sitting in one of the plastic chairs sipping on his coffee, someone sat down right next to him. Rory smelled the man's old clothes and the overwhelming whiff of cheap liquor seeping out of his mouth as he breathed unevenly. Rory turned to look at him. The man had a big grin on his face and was staring right at him.

"Roy," he said, bursting out in a laugh, "Where the hell you get to?"

It was Jake. Rory was suddenly elated to see someone he knew, and almost gave him a hug, but the odour held him back.

"Can you spring for another of those?" asked Jake eyeing the coffee.

"Sure," Rory stuck his hands in his pocket, came up with a loony and some change, and passed it to him.

"Yeah, I bin drinking a bit, helps keep me warm ... say where you staying? I got a place, if youse need somewhere to crash."

At about the same time, Roxanne Mallory had called and woken up Henning telling him what had happened. "Jesson must have gotten on a bus or something and is now somewhere in the east side of Vancouver."

Henning cursed, then told her to come and pick him up at the hotel. They drove around for some time trying to locate Rory. Neither knew the city, and the streets were confusing to them, particularly all the concrete barricades blocking half of the side-streets. The computer screen indicated he was down a back street near Commercial Drive. But when they arrived, the street appeared deserted. Both Henning and Mallory took out flashlights and walked up and down the sector where the screen indicated he was, checking the darkened areas that the street lights didn't cover.

Henning put his finger to his lips and whispered and pointed, "He must be in this dumpster."

On cue they both leaped up and shone their lights inside. There was no one there. But sitting on top of part of what might have once been a desk lay a black wallet. Roxanne lifted it up, examining it.

"Fuck!" Was all Henning could say.

"How'd he know there was a bug in it?" asked Mallory, more to herself than to her partner.

For the next few days Rory followed Jake around, learning how to panhandle, Jake trying to teach him which marks to hit, and which "wouldn't give you a nickel to save their souls." Jake knew where all the free food was given out and when, and he knew which restaurants threw out food that was retrievable and edible. Rory knew very soon that this sort of life was completely alien to him, and he was way out of his element. When Jake was sober, that is in the mornings, he was quiet, gruff and uncommunicative. After a few drinks, usually cheap Chinese wine, he became eloquent for a period of two or three hours, until slowly the verbosity degenerated into incoherence. Jake took a liking to Rory because he seemed like an honest guy, who was just down on his luck. A situation that had happened to Jake several years earlier. One that had not changed. When lucid, Jake urged Rory to, "Go back to whatever the fuck it was you were doing." But he realized after some time that Rory really couldn't remember much.

"Well, I can tell you one thing, son. You were never around this neck of the woods. That's for damn sure."

At night Jake took Rory down to where he and some other homeless pals had found a hide-away by the rail yards in an old abandoned cabin. As long as they were reasonably quiet the rail yard police never bothered them. This is where Rory met the Hawk. Prompted by a jug of wine Rory and Jake had acquired, the Hawk entertained them with wit and what he called his Native wisdom — he was part Mi'kMaq — for half the night. He had spent fourteen years in prison for a murder he did not commit, and he told the listeners, who'd probably heard all this before but none the less seemed enraptured, of the fights he used to have with the guards and some of the prisoners because he was considered a tough guy.

"A tough bloke, all right," he said, impersonating John Lennon. "They all want a piece of the Hawk. Ha, ha, ha .. One, two, three ... What do you see at the end of the day..." And sang the first verse of A Little Help From My Friends.

"And when I came to Vancouver, all the cops wanted to have it out with me, right back over there in Gastown. Up that alley. Blood Alley they call it. I was the big test for all the rookies, who'd come down and try and punch me out. 'Course usually there was a few of them and eventually I admit they did ... but not before I'd bloodied their noses somewhat." The Hawk switched to Winston Churchill, "England expects every man to do his duty ... hahaha ... I guess I done my duty enough down there. 'Course they leave me alone now ..."

"Well, the cops have changed," said Jake.

"Nah, the cops haven't changed, they're still assholes. They just pick on the crackheads and Indians now." Everyone, including Rory without really knowing why, burst out laughing.

Jake had been a disc jockey in Halifax before being arrested for the murder. Rory got the impression he knew who really did it, but the Hawk wasn't the type to rat on someone.

To hell with that, Rory thought. It isn't snitching when it's murder. Fourteen years! Rory had trouble understanding that. He admired this guy, who even at fifty-five or so looked like he could still fight his way out of most scraps. Big arms, big chest, a face that had a tough John Lennon profile but with a broken nose, and a sense of humour like a delinquent teenage schoolboy. Although he was sleeping on a hard plywood floor that night, Rory slept like a child. The first real sleep he'd had in weeks.

Rory awoke to the sound of locomotives shunting boxcars merely twenty feet from the old shack they had slept in. His eyes gazed around the cabin. Several men and one woman lay prone in various positions on the floor. Some had ratty-looking sleeping bags, others had covered themselves with blankets. Maybe because the night before they'd been drinking he hadn't noticed the stench that filled his nostrils now. It was so pungent he decided to get the hell out. Besides, although it was still early, it was a lovely day and he wanted to explore some more.

He wandered west along the waterfront, as best he was able to, until he came to a large park. This is Stanley Park, he said to himself. Good, at least part of my memory is coming back.

He walked around the path on the south side of Lost Lagoon. He stopped by a huge oak tree, the branches of which dangled over the swampy water. High up at a fork in the tree's trunk two young raccoons were watching him with what he felt was a sense of curiosity. Their fur seemed to glimmer, and their eyes were full of light and intelligence. Like a couple of telepathic twins, they both climbed down the tree front-first, in unison, and came towards him. They stopped about three feet in front of him, and at the same moment both brought up their right paws, or hands, Rory thought. He saw that their little black hands were either begging him for some nuts or giving him some sort of raccoon welcome.

He smiled, and as he had nothing to give the animals he smiled again, then moved on continuing his walk around the lagoon. Lost Lagoon, he thought. How could it be lost? It's right in the middle of downtown. I'm fucking lost, he thought — not this big pond. He stopped suddenly when he saw a small black animal come toward him. What the hell is that? he asked himself.

It's a skunk? God. He thought of running off, but the

skunk was so sleek, and looked so harmless, and it even seemed to have a smile on its face. Rory stood his ground. The skunk came right up to him, stopped a mere foot away. Rory crouched down to smile at it. When he did so the skunk came even closer and gave him a kiss on his cheek. At first Rory was stunned, and then he started laughing. He gave the skunk a little pat on its head, then ambled down a path through the forest. He remembered, vaguely, being in these woods before, and continued because he felt safe.

The unconscious fear, almost terror, that he had felt in the city streets evaporated, and he found himself walking down sparser footpaths, until finally he was in a grove where the sun's rays barely came through the treed canopy above. He sat on some dried moss, and stared up through the leaves of some coniferous bushes. He became hypnotized by the dancing sunrays, and also became aware of the sound of birds chirping. The more he relaxed, the more harmonious the sounds became, until he was listening to choruses of sonatas. He lay down in the moss, his mind at peace for the first time … since when? In thinking about the past Rory immediately lost his mood of tranquillity. He sat up abruptly as a horde of horrific visions screamed through his consciousness like sirens. They came so fast he could only retain vague images, but one such memory seemed like a frightening painting he had seen in an art gallery when he was a child. A Goya? A shiver ran through him. He got up and walked off in the direction he had come. It was a Goya he'd seen in a gallery in New York. The Museum of Modern Art? He'd been looking at it, when suddenly he saw the horror of the work. He was ten years old, and it had scared him to his soul.

As he came out of the grove, he saw several crows diving like fighter pilots onto some animal. The animal was scurrying down the trail trying to avoid the sharp beaks, and claws of the crows. As the animal turned its head Rory could see it was an older raccoon with only one eye, and a rangy, indistinct tail. It had the appearance of a marauding bandit. Another crow swooped down aiming at the one good eye; the egg stealer dashed into the bushes.

The crows flew back up in a large cedar tree, squawking in triumph. That's why they call them a murder of crows, he thought. Funny, he hadn't thought about such things for years. Or had he? He could hardly remember anything. But the Museum of Modern Art was a start. He'd been to New York. Jake had said he had a slight Yankee accent. What the hell was he doing here then?

Chapter Two

It was on the morning of the fourth day. Rory and Jake were panhandling. Wolfgang was walking down the street when Jake approached him. Wolf reached into his pocket for some change, and then noticed Rory behind the old guy.

"Rory! Where the hell've you been?" he asked, both amazed and pleased to see him again.

Rory looked at him nervously and unsure of himself. "You know me?"

"What the hell have you been smoking? Jenny's? Last month? You were living there. Remember our conversations about media concentration?" Wolfgang was puzzled. It didn't look like he was joking and Rory acted a hell of a lot different than he had before. No self confidence at all. He looked scared.

"I'm afraid I don't. What's your name?"

"Wolfgang." He looked over at Jake to see his reaction, but Jake just nodded his head ambiguously.

"This is Jake." Rory said, seeing them exchange looks.

"Pleasure," said Jake coming forward. "Can you spare us a little change, friend. Roy and I are dead broke. I'll be honest … we want to buy a bottle."

Wolfgang, for a change, was lost for words. "Sure." He

turned to Rory. "Rory, Jenny says you left all your stuff at her place, why don't you come with me. You been on a drunk or something?"

"I guess so, I really don't remember much at all. I woke up a couple of days ago in the park with this fellow ... I can't seem to remember much at all." Rory hesitated. He was thinking that Wolfgang looked like a friend, someone he might know. "But you know me, right? You knew my name."

"Look, I'll take you to Jenny's. Then you'll remember."

"Maybe that'll help." He paused again and looked at Jake. He could see that he'd have to leave him, and felt a little guilty about that. He turned to Wolfgang. "Jenny? Maybe I'll remember her. Is she my wife?"

Wolf had to laugh. "No, you just met her a few weeks back."

"I think I have a wife. God this is terrible. I think I had an accident. I seem to remember doctors ..."

Wolfgang was concerned for the first time. He looked over at Jake, and realized that Jake had probably helped him out. He pulled out twenty dollars.

"Here, go and buy a decent bottle of Bordeaux ... Oh, whatever you want."

That brought a smile to Jake. "A gentleman. You look after Roy here, he's good people." Jake grinned at Rory, winked and headed down the street to the liquor store. Wolfgang put his arm on Rory's shoulder. "Here, we go the other way," and led him up the street.

They continued to walk up Main Street, when Wolfgang became aware of a man following them. It was Henning, who had finally found Rory that morning and, dressed like a vagrant, was keeping him under surveillance, until they could plant another bug on him.

Wolfgang tapped Rory on his shoulder. "Don't look now, but there's a guy following us."

Rory looked anyway. "That guy? I've seen him before. He's just a hobo."

"Yeah, wearing $300 shoes." Wolf said sarcastically. "Listen we can't go home yet. You want a beer?"

Rory looked worried, but something in Wolfgang's demeanor reassured him. "Okay."

"Follow me."

Wolf suddenly took off. Rory was startled, then caught on and caught up. Henning, not sure what to do, resisted running but upped his pace and followed trying to keep them in sight. When they had turned a corner, he started to run too.

Wolfgang barrelled through the doors of the Main Hotel, followed closely by Rory, who glanced back as the door was closing to see if he could detect Henning. He thought he couldn't, and turning into the room was overwhelmed at what he saw. Wolfgang was walking ahead of him as if he owned the place, saying Hi to practically everyone in the large, dismal bar-room. Rory was reminded of some gangster movie he'd seen where the camera followed someone into a bar of wiseguys. Only these guys looked more like bikers.

As Wolfgang charged past the tables where four or five people were seated at most of them, Rory followed in a daze. What on Earth am I doing here? he thought. I've only seen this sort of place in movies. Wiseguys! that was the name of the movie. No. It was Goodfellas. Wolfgang commandeered a table, waved to the waiter and sat down so that he was facing the door. Rory sat down unsteadily opposite him.

"Want to bet that bum follows us in here?" Wolfgang asked.

"I don't have any money," Rory said checking his pockets.

Then realized it was an expression. "Why would he be following me?"

"Don't worry about money, I'm buying. Listen, I've got a lot to tell you, but that'll have to wait till we lose this dude. Don't turn round again, here he is."

This time Rory took his time in turning, looked around the bar, and, as Henning entered seeming to be a bit pissed, he turned back at Wolfgang.

"Buy why?"

Wolfgang shrugged.

"This place looks familiar." Rory added looking over at the pool tables.

"It should, I brought you here once before." Rory didn't know what to reply, but when a waiter dropped two pints on the table, he was startled by the abruptness.

Wolfgang laid ten dollars on the terry-clothed table, sat back in his chair smiling at the waiter. "Keep the change, Serge."

"Thanks Wolf. How's it going? Haven't seen you for awhile."

"It goes. Is Tiny in?"

"Yeah, he's over there playing pool."

"How could I miss him." Wolfgang looked over at the pool tables, Tiny, a monster of three hundred aggressive pounds was lining up a shot, making the cue look not a hell of a lot bigger than a toothpick.

"Look Rory, drink your beer. We'll shoot the shit for a bit, and then we're going to split. Quick. So be ready when I tell you."

Rory looked puzzled. Things were going about two hundred miles an hour too fast for him. "Okay." Rory gazed around again at the customers. "How come you hang out in such dives?"

Wolfgang gave a small chuckle and went into one of his routines as he stood up. "Because the poor are the salt of the Earth. They may be a bit smelly, but they're good people. The poor live in a politically marginalized urban jungle, which is under constant surveillance by the state — by the police, like that asshole over there, probably," he nodded towards Henning. "Don't look!" Rory, who was just about to, froze. "The police protect the class systems operating to keep the poor poor. And the rich shall inherit the earth ..."

"Isn't it the meek?" Rory asked timidly.

"No that was a mistranslation in the St. James version. It's the rich who'll get it all by buying up all the real estate. The whole idea of private property is suspect, of course. It means, for example, Native Indians, who never conceived of private property, become tenants in their own land. Eventually we all will be tenants to feudal corporate landlords. And the corporations don't have to lobby the government anymore. They are the government."

Rory had been watching this performance, gaping. He was also slightly embarrassed as some of the other patrons started looking over, laughing. "Now I remember you," Rory said. "You were talking like this before. I can't remember where."

"Jenny's."

"Jenny's?" Rory was losing it again.

"I'm taking you there as soon as we lose 'Smiley' over there. Wait here, I'll be back and when I do, get ready to run."

Wolfgang walked over to the pool tables. Tiny noticed him coming up and gave him a big grin. "Wolf, how the fuck you doing?"

"Nothing a few pipes of opium couldn't cure. Hey Tiny, see that creep sitting over there in the old raincoat?" Wolfgang motioned with his head subtly. Henning was in the middle of ordering a drink. Tiny looked at the guy.

"Yeah, so?"

Wolfgang winked at him. "He's a faggot and he's been drooling over you ever since he sat down. Last week he tried to grab my balls in the can." Tiny got the message, and glared over at Henning, who wasn't looking. Tiny moved between Wolfgang and headed over to Henning's table.

"Hey you, you little piece of shit, what're you looking at?"

Henning looked up, confused. "Me? Nothing." He wasn't used to being treated this way, but Tiny looked like he was a street fighter, and Henning dreaded fighting them as they weren't predictable. Before Henning could think more about the matter, Tiny rushed in and hammered him. Henning felt his nose break. In the background, Wolfgang led Rory out the back door. The last image Wolfgang saw was Henning getting knocked onto the beer-wet floor, unconscious.

"What'd I tell you, Rory? Salt of the Earth." He said as they walked up the alley.

Chapter Three

For several days Jenny and Wolfgang tried to help Rory remember at least the little they knew about him. Both of them were the kind of people who compulsively help others in need, so although they didn't really know Rory that well it was beholden on them to help him. Jenny also had grown attached to him. She found him sexy and intelligent, even though he was obviously from the right side of town. She also believed that he was in big shit with some big shits, as she told Wolfie.

She was initially surprised, of course, to see Rory, and shocked too to see him in such a condition. Not only was his whole appearance different and shabby, but he had none of the self-confidence and bearing that he used to. She immediately guessed that he'd been in an accident, and when Wolf told her he'd lost his memory she began to tell Rory how she had met him. Rory, while he felt he'd been here before and that he knew Jenny, really couldn't remember any specifics, so he sat and listened, like a little kid. The three sat in the living room while Jenny went over the period since they had known each other. She brought out a bag and laid some items on the table.

"This is yours, Rory," she brought out a lap-top and put it

on the table, then a Sony professional digital audio recorder, "and so is this and you had been taping your thoughts. You were some sort of TV producer ..."

"TV!" said Rory, "I thought so." He said it in such a naive voice it was like a child saying he was going to be a movie star.

"Frankly, since you disappeared I've been snooping, and I've listened to a couple of these cassettes. This one," she held one up, "is your recollections of what was happening just before you met me." She put it in the recorder and pressed play. There was silence for a moment until Rory's voice came on. It sounded quite different. Much more self-assured.

"I have to admit I was choked up. I'd fallen into the naive belief that we were family at CATV, I guess from watching too much of our own friendly news coverage team. To be dumped like this without a hearing, without at least a phone call from Al hurt more than anything that had happened except Suzanne's death.

As soon as I got on the highway I pressed the accelerator to the floor, and cruised into the outside lane. I put on Herbie Hancock's Dis is da Drum and aimed the car downtown. My eyes were focused on the lanes ahead, my mind was churning over and over being unceremoniously kicked out of the TV station, and I was speeding way too fast. The music was beginning to soothe my murderous anger, so I slowed down somewhat. It took me several minutes to realize I was being followed. It started as a feeling of paranoia. I exited the highway and headed for the east-side. As I checked the rear-view mirror again it seemed to me that a white delivery van was tailing me. I turned right, then right, then right again — back on the same street, and still the white van was two or three cars behind. In downtown Gastown, where traffic slows to pedestrian speed, I made a left up a one-way street. The wrong way. That's when I knew for sure I was being followed and they obviously didn't care that I knew. I sped the opposite way down Cordova Street and then headed towards the Skytrain at Main. I finally lost them at a red light I ran, and thinking to lose them altogether, I parked the car, grabbed my bag and headed up the street to the Skytrain. At the top of the stairs I looked back to see if they were in sight. I couldn't see the white van, and it didn't look like anyone was following. I gave a huge sigh of relief. The adrenaline had my whole system in overdrive. I placed myself behind a group of commuters and waited for the next train.

I'd only once before been on the Skytrain and that was to do a news story on it several years back. I found myself heading out of town, not that it mattered much, I had no idea what I was doing. It wasn't until the next stop that I noticed someone in the next car glaring at me through the window, talking excitedly on a cell phone. As soon as the train stopped he got out and came into my car, and walked towards me. I've seen hoods before. I've met so-called Mafia mobsters. I've interviewed some of them. This guy looked like a low-level hit-man. As he approached he pushed his jacket away to show me his gun. And I totally panicked. I found myself headed for the door, with Fuck-face trying to head me off, without breaking into a run. I got to the door first, turned, and out of some insane instinctive reaction kicked him. If I was aiming for the guy's nuts I missed, but it got his thigh enough for him to fall back, while my legs took off carrying me at sprinting speed along the platform.

I didn't look back. I got to the stairs and ran down skipping every other stair. I didn't even look as I got to the street. I just kept going. It wasn't until I'd turned down a residential side-street that I stopped enough to check behind. At first I was relieved. There was no one following. Only I was wrong. Although he was panting and limping somewhat on the leg I'd kicked, Fuck-face was only a half a block back. And he'd seen me. I sprinted the entire next block, but the sudden exertion gave me stomach cramps, and I stopped, stooped over for a minute to get my breath back. I knew I had to find a taxi, or even better a cop, or ... as I looked up I saw that the front door of the house was open. Without really thinking I ran up the stairs, let myself in through the half-open door, and as quietly as I could, closed it.

"Is that you, Wolf?" came a voice from what smelled like the kitchen.

I couldn't think of a thing to say. God, what if she thinks I'm a rapist, I thought. As I was trying to think of something, a dark-haired girl's face and neck appeared in the hallway.

"What the hell are you doing here?" she asked in a threatening manner.

"There's someone with a gun after me." I told her, trying to act cool.

"He's not in a blue uniform is he?" Her whole body came into frame, and all of it looked good. Her tone had changed. She looked down at the bag I was carrying. I looked for the first time into her big brown eyes.

"No, some Mafia guys are after me."

Jenny — I found out later that was her name — moved, glided really, over to the window which had a half-opened, green, French blind covering it. She slowly closed the blinds as she looked out on the street.

"Hey, you're right. One creepy-looking guy just went by."

She looked over at me with a little more belief than she had earlier. I spread my hands like one of those old Jewish comedians that used to do the old talk shows. I thought of something clever to say.

"I never lie to pretty women." She grimaced. "I'm sorry, your door was open, and I figured I could hide for a bit." I said rather lamely. Something like that.

Jenny, I guess, seeing that I was shaken, offered me a drink, which I gladly accepted. She had some home-made wine, that she brought out of the fridge, while I put down my bag and peeked through the blinds.

Whoever had been following me was now at the end of the street, at an intersection and was looking both right, left, north and south. But he didn't look back here, which I figured was very good news. I closed the blinds as Jenny came back with a couple of glasses of red vino.

She gave me a glass, then checked through the blinds herself. The guy was gone, so we sat down and introduced ourselves. She told me she was a dancer, I said I worked in television.

"So tell me. What's this all about, Rory?" There was a hint of sexuality in her voice that I decided to file away for a later hour. So I told her most of what had happened. It took a bottle of wine and a joint to finish. I don't know why I told her so much, but Jenny — not only was she gorgeous, but gregarious too ... well who wouldn't tell her everything? I'd never been so physically attracted to anyone before, and Jenny seemed to have no inhibitions. She suggested I stay for the afternoon, and I couldn't bring myself to say no. After awhile she had me up dancing, then one thing led to another ... and not that much later we were up in her bedroom having the best sex I'd ever had.

When we had dressed and returned to the living room, I checked my phone messages. There was one from Pete Fraser.

"I just talked to Turnbull. There's something very strange going on. The registration was stolen from Turnbull's and probably the gun too. I'll call back, or call me. I also e-mailed you the details."

Jenny's expression changed. She certainly believed me now. I asked if she'd mind if I called him back on my cell. She said, fine.

But when I talked to Pete's office, the receptionist was somehow hesitant. I told her I was a friend and she put me through to his editor. Pete was dead, she told me quite frankly. I was shocked, then extremely guilty. Shit. How did it happen? I asked. She told me it was a heart attack. Somehow I was relieved. But that didn't make much sense either, Pete was in great health, didn't smoke.

I guess the editor sensed my astonishment. She asked me how well I knew Pete. I told her we were very old friends, and I had just seen him recently.

"Well, Rory," she said. "Right now it's all innuendo. His wife's a doctor, she saw blood and a needle mark on his neck. She's having it investigated as a possible homicide. You know, he told me yesterday morning he was on to something a bit dangerous. Know anything about that, Rory?"

I told her I didn't. Told her I was real sorry about Pete, and hung up.

"Pete's been murdered." I told Jenny, who'd been listening with rapt attention. "It has to do with me. Shit! I should never have asked him to help. God-damn. Jesus Christ!" First Suzanne, now my old best friend. I was furious with myself, and frustrated that I had no clue what was happening.

"Rory. It wasn't your fault. Don't blame yourself," she said.

"Yeah. It was." I told her, searching through my notebook to get Freedman's number in Connecticut. I pressed a button and the phone rang.

I asked for Lieutenant Freedman. I looked over at Jenny while I waited and gave her a kind of pathetic wink. When Freedman came on the line, I asked if there had been any further developments in my father's case. Freedman seemed annoyed that I brought it up, and said that there hadn't been, and it was still listed as "an accidental death."

I told him about Pete Fraser, whom he had heard of. I tried

to make a link between the suspicious needle marks on Pete, and the ones that had been found on my father.

Freedman seemed to think I was some conspiracy theorist, so I told him about Suzanne's death as well, and the burglaries.

That seemed to make Freedman sound a little more serious, and he told me that he would contact the police department looking after Fraser's death — if they were.

I hung up, realizing there was no point in pursuing this with him. When he asked for my number I gave him my home one, as I was beginning to think maybe he had been paid off by whoever was behind these deaths.

I turned to Jenny. She came over and kissed me, then offered to let me stay the night. I accepted for two reasons. One, I was becoming very paranoid. And two, she was extremely lovely.

I decided before I forgot all this important shit that'd been happening since I left New York, the details anyway, I should record it all — which I'm doing, including the voice-mail of Pete's — on this DAT recorder I had not returned to CATV. Fuck them!"

Chapter Four

Jenny stopped the tape. "So someone was after you. Your girl friend, Suzanne, was murdered. You were, or are, a suspect ..." She realized she was being a bit tough. "But we both believed what you told us, didn't we Wolf?"

"I'd met you before," Wolf said.

"Anyway, after that you stayed here ..." She began to relate what happened over the next few days, things that weren't on Rory's tapes.

She began with how her and Rory were in her kitchen preparing dinner. More to the point, Jenny was making a mouth-watering Oriental sea-food spread and Rory was cutting up the ingredients of a very interesting looking salad. Jenny was filling Rory in on the living arrangements in her house, as she chopped up some chili pepper into tiny little red dots. The house was an east-end old-timer with three bedrooms upstairs, and a large living room, kitchen, and dining room down.

"You see, Wolfgang's just a friend. He rents a room, but seeing as we're friends he has the run of the place."

"He looks familiar." Rory said, not sure whether to believe her or not about the relationship. At the same moment Wolfgang traipsed into the kitchen with two empty glasses, opened the fridge, took out a large bottle of wine and started filling the glasses.

"That smells wonderful," he told Jenny, as she stirred the wok and added the sea food to the steaming vegetables. She smiled and looked over at Rory.

"Why don't you go and join Wolf and Sara? I can finish easier without a bloody mob in this little kitchen."

"Sure." Rory grabbed his glass of wine and followed Wolfgang into the antique dining room.

"What kind of television do you do, Rory?" asked Wolfgang as they sat down.

"None right now," he realized. "I was doing documentaries up until yesterday."

"Wolfgang makes films," volunteered Sara, looking up at Wolf as if he were some kind of hero.

"Political performance art," she told Rory. When he looked confused she elaborated. "You know, following politicians around with a camera and asking them personal questions about their sex lives."

Rory gave a polite chuckle. He wasn't sure whether this was performance art, which he hated, or Rick Mercer, who he rolled over. Jenny burst into the room with two steaming bowls of food and placed them in the centre of the table, before immediately returning to the kitchen. She reappeared bringing another two bowls, one the salad, the other a chow mein dish, then sat down.

"Jenny, that looks so delicious," Sara said enthusiastically, but with a lisp that made Rory look at her closely. He lowered his eyes to her breasts, which were not apparent, as she was wearing a loose fluffy sweater.

"I will vouch for Jenny's cuisine," said Wolfgang smiling oddly at Rory, raising his wine glass. "Since I moved in here six months ago I've put on ten pounds. Look at it." He stood up clutching a piece of his fatty waist. Jenny and Sara laughed.

"I've known Wolfie for … frigging years." Jenny said toasting back. "He's weird. But at least he's funny weird. Aren't you, Wolf?"

Wolf made a curiously exact look of Charlie Chaplin looking innocent, then digging into the food. The Gold Rush, Rory remembered. Sara automatically went into a fit of hysterics. Jenny smiled, and Rory was in awe. Jenny looked over at Rory. "I don't know this guy at all, but he's a TV producer, or something. Hey, maybe he can promote your book?" She gave a familiar smile to Wolfgang.

"He just told me he was finished with television." He glanced at Rory, who was putting a mouthful of sweet and sour prawn in his mouth. "What's this book she's talking about?" Rory asked after chewing for a moment.

"First let me tell you a story I'm working on … maybe a screenplay. It's a true story about a blind artist …" Wolfgang anticipated the interruption.

"A blind artist?" Jenny started to crack up. Sara following suit.

"Why not a blind artist … there's deaf composers … Anyway he paints little canvases and sells them on street corners for twenty dollars. One day an art critic buys one, raves about his new find, and all of a sudden the guy's paintings are selling for $20,000. So he gets an eye operation …"

"And…?" asked Jenny amidst laughter.

"Well, he looks at his paintings…"

"And…?" both Jenny and Sara said.

"And he's horrified. Completely horrified that he could paint such awful crap, so he burns them all. And starts painting still life … " Wolfgang paused for effect, then looked around the table, "Which he can only sell for $20."

By this time everyone was laughing. Even Wolfgang was having trouble keeping a straight face, because by this time it was obvious he had made up the whole thing on the spur of the moment.

"What's the moral there?" Rory managed to say.

"Ah, it's too complicated." Wolfgang waved him off, good-naturedly.

"Wolf, that's funny, but that's not the book I meant." She turned to Rory. "Wolfie hasn't been the same since he got whacked over the head in Seattle in '99. Wolf, you know the book I mean." She said looking at him more seriously, then picking up some chow mien with her chopsticks

"You mean, 'Survival of the Fattest'?"

"Good title!" said Rory still laughing .

"So far I've sold a hundred and two copies. That's a best seller in the east side." Wolfgang looked around the table grinning. Then dropped the smile and looked at Rory more seriously. "It's a look at the effects of globalization on several fronts. I couldn't find a publisher, so I did it myself."

"I'd like to read it. When I get out of this mess." Rory offered. Jenny picked up on that and told the others that some people, probably Mafia, were chasing Rory.

"Well, it couldn't be the Mafia," Wolfgang said emphatically.

"Why not?" Jenny asked, slightly hostile.

"We'd all be dead by now." Wolf laughed loudly, but the others all had a touch of nervousness in their laughs. He stood up and with a theatrical voice said:

"'I suppose these ginks who say that everything breaks even in this old dump of a world of ours argue that because the rich man gets ice in summer, and the poor man gets it in winter, things are breaking even for both. Maybe so, but I'll swear I can't see it that way.' Bat Masterson wrote that. They were the last words he ever wrote as columnist for the New York

Morning Telegraph — a Randolph Hearst paper, believe it or not — it about describes what I'm writing about."

"Who's fucking Randolf Hurts?" asked Jenny. "C'mon you guys, lighten up." She looked over at Sara for support. She wasn't into politics much either and nodded back.

"You don't have to listen Jenny. Let me talk to Rory, it's not often you pick up intelligent guys ..."

Wolf hadn't finished when Jenny interrupted with, "Well fuck you too. And I didn't pick him up, he barged right in here all by himself."

"Yeah I did, she's a lifesaver ...."

"Thank you Rory. You got a problem with that, Wolfgang?

Wolfgang laughed, Rory joining in. She isn't an intellectual, but she's real, he thought.

"So me and Sara have decided that we're going to the Das Beat warehouse party. You guys get your acts together and we'll go do ours." Jenny said, turning and leading Sara towards the bathroom.

"Living in the same house with Jen, you gotta take your own space." Wolfgang said, winking at Rory, after they were out of ear shot. "What was I was saying ?"

"Bat Masterson." Rory remembered.

"They've made I don't know how many films about Wyatt Earp, and none about Bat Masterson. Wyatt Earp, like most American heroes, was a fucking scoundrel. Plus they practically murdered the Clantons. Bat at least had some integrity," Wolfgang finished.

"Like working for Hearst?" One of Rory's favourite subjects was media monopolies.

Wolfgang put his finger in the air and scored on an imaginary board. "Score one for the TV guy! Masterson gambled, drank, played the ponies. He did what the hell he wanted to. He wrote about the crooked politicians, the big fixes ... He set up one of the last bare-knuckle boxing fights — Sullivan and Gentleman Jim Corbett."

"That'd be a hell of a movie." Rory gave him a quick toast of his glass before taking a swallow.

"And he was in one of the last Commanche wars. A handful of buffalo hunters against a hundred Native Indians. It'd be a great movie." Wolfgang looked at Rory his eyes gleaming. "Lots of action anyway."

"You guys ready? We already phoned the cab," Jenny yelled coming down the stairs.

Wolfgang, Rory and Jenny walked with beer cans in their hands trying to find a table at the warehouse party. There were hundreds of young people milling about, talking excitedly at tables. There was a make-shift stage where a couple of young men were setting things up for a performance. The music was hip-hop and loud to Rory's jazz attuned ears. Some cute thing at a table with a few chairs left waved to Jenny and they made their way over and sat down. While Jenny talked to her friend, Rory leaned over to Wolfgang's ear.

"This place is different," he said, realizing this was a whole other side of Vancouver he'd rarely seen.

"You don't know how different."

"What happened to Sara?"

Wolfgang rolled his head back and laughed. At the same time from the stage came an announcement.

"Ladies and gentlemen, boys and girls, girls and girls, and boys and boys ... direct from Las Vegas, where she won the most talented singer award at the Miss USA Chicks with Dicks contest ... here's Sara V."

Rory looked in amazement as Sara waltzed on stage,

winked to their table and to the accompaniment of recorded music broke into the first verse of All of Me. Rory didn't know what to do and for almost the entire song he just gazed at Sara, except when she looked at him, then his eyes lowered pretending to check out someone in the crowd. When he finally did look back at Wolfgang, he still looked like he was laughing.

"Here take one of these, it'll loosen you up," he said passing Rory a pill.

"What is it?"

In response Wolfgang just popped one in his mouth. Rory thought, What the hell, and did the same thing.

After about an hour of various acts — they weren't all gay, and Rory liked one of the bands — a Cuban combo — immensely. So immensely he found himself dancing with Jenny doing some kind of Rumba. After that things became progressively vague as the Ecstasy and beer took complete effect.

He suddenly found himself on a stage, doing a play which incorporated several old films starting with a scene from Cat on a Hot Tin Roof, but it had been changed for maximum laughs, which he found he was getting with every line. He was playing opposite Elizabeth Taylor, or maybe a drag queen playing her, who got increasingly angry over the upstaging until she finally demanded the director use his understudy. Rory protested that he was ad-libbing because no one had given him a script.

Rory left the stage in embarrassment, sat down in the audience, and was astounded when his understudy turned out to be Mick Jagger who had risen out of the audience to take his place. Mick was sporting a mustache, and was cheered as he stood up. Then someone said, Hey Rory and as he looked around everyone was laughing at him. Laughing loudest, with his Joker's grin, sitting right next to him was Jack Nicholson. As Rory looked to his other side there was Robert De Niro chuckling into his hand, then put an arm around him slapping him on the back.

"Don't worry Rory, we all get stage fright."

"I didn't have stage fright," he protested. "No one gave me a script." At that both De Niro and Nicholson cracked up, and as Rory looked around he realized there were many famous people and they were all laughing at him, even Liz Taylor and Mick Jagger, who seemed to be doing a completely different play by then.

Rory woke up. He started to jump up when he didn't recognize anything, and that woke up Jenny, who was lying next to him in her bed.

"Whatz up?" she murmured sleepily. It took a moment for Rory to reply.

"How did we get here? Last I remember was at that party."

Jenny's eyes opened and she looked at him quizzically. "So you don't remember making love?" She turned, grabbed a pillow and playfully hit his head with it.

"What the hell was it Wolf gave me?"

"Oh, now it makes sense. I should have warned you never take anything from Wolfie. He pops pills like they say Hendrix used to."

"I just had a bizarre dream. I thought we were still at the club, then it turned into a cabaret theatre ... I was in a play with Elizabeth Taylor ..."

"What was she like?"

"What was she *like*?"

"Yeah was she young or like she is now — an aging looking drag queen?"

"She was a bitch. She fired me from the play." Jenny started laughing. When Rory looked confused, she said, "You're taking it so seriously... it's only a dream," and laughed again.

Rory wasn't so sure. His dreams had become unusually vivid and prophetic, and he still couldn't remember anything between dancing at the warehouse club and waking up. He'd been drunk before, he'd done mushrooms, hash and other psychedelic drugs, but he'd never completely blacked out like that — he'd always remember something. And that last dream seemed so real. Of course it couldn't have been, but ...

"I've been thinking ..." said Jenny realizing Rory was starting to brood.

Rory immediately changed moods. "I know I could hear your brain cells churning,"

"No, seriously. Why would the Mafia be after your dad's files, or whatever?"

"Maybe he had something on them, who knows? But I couldn't find anything at all that would incriminate anyone. It doesn't make a whole lot of sense."

"So what are you gonna do?" Jenny asked, sitting up, looking dead serious.

"I don't know, but I can't stay here, I don't want to involve you in this."

Jenny gave him a look that said she was already involved. For some time they were silent.

"So tell me about yourself," Rory asked, to break the silence and because he had been curious about her from the beginning. Perhaps because he had spent his adult life questioning people, when it came to personal relationships he tended to be the opposite.

"What's to tell?" Jenny shrugged.

"Well, where are you from?"

"C'mon I don't want to talk serious."

"I told you my story. Your turn." Rory slurred his words,

and laughed because he found the sound of his own voice funny. Jenny looked at him strangely, and her attitude changed from frivolous to sober.

"Well, I never had any of the advantages you did. Okay, to begin with I did maybe, but I was too young to remember. I spent my childhood with relatives."

"What happened to your mother?"

"It's funny, I never talked about this before. I don't want to now, neither."

"Did she die when you were young?"

"No." Jenny turned to look at Rory. She had tears in her eyes. "No, she didn't. And she had a lot of class — her parents were rich. I was born in the Caribbean. But I was illegitimate. My real dad was the family gardener, he was black. 'Course I never found that out till I was sweet sixteen, and had lived with my uncle who had been fucking me from the time I was about twelve."

Rory suddenly sobered up. "What?"

"That's why I never talk about it. Funny when I get drunk I still think about him. In fact I think I must've loved him." She looked Rory closely in the eyes. "Isn't that strange?"

Rory supposed it was, and he'd heard some strange accounts in his days as a reporter.

"What happened to your father? What about your mother? She just left you?"

"I never saw my father. He was either run off or maybe killed I don't know. My mother? I don't have a mother as far as I'm concerned. She never saw me, got married to some respectable plantation owner's son. I was never mentioned. At least according to my aunt. That's my aunt on my father's side who got me away from the uncle and brought me to Canada. She's the one I consider my mother."

Rory was holding back tears. It was one of the saddest stories he'd ever heard. Yet this woman was so vivacious, so generous. He noticed she had tears in her eyes too, and reached his arms around her and hugged her for a long, long time.

Chapter Five

"You spent another week or so here," Jenny said, her hand on the tape recorder, "and we went to clubs and had a good time," she smiled at him seductively, but Rory didn't respond. Anyway this is where the tape continues ..." She pressed play and Rory's old voice came on.

"*Hiding out is not as exciting as the movies make it out to be. If it weren't for the fact that Jenny is so fascinating and vibrant, I'd take my chances and go back to my condo. The police had told me to stay in Vancouver, and so far I have. Technically I'm still a suspect. I made a call from a phone booth to check in with the cop, Marshall, and the word was that the case is still open. Part of me wants to go to New York to see if I can dig anything up, and maybe find out something about Pete's murder, and at least pass on my sympathies to his family. But to do so would get the Canadian police after me, which might then bring in the FBI. I am also to the point where I don't think Freedman believed me; but he would have had to suspect something with Pete Fraser. I tried calling him from the phone booth too, but I couldn't connect, and obviously couldn't leave a number.*

Wolfgang, who's been at many of the WTO protests, thinks I have every right to be paranoid. He sees a great conspiracy behind

globalization that is taking the world back to the laissez-faire cap-
italism of the 19th century, where health, education and other
social programs will disappear or be privatized; but his biggest beef
is the way the corporations treat the environment and are polluting
world-wide. I agree with him there. Unfortunately there's some-
thing wrong with the way corporations are set up. Their entire focus
is usually on short-term profit, so items like pollution, or killing
animals to the point of extinction doesn't show on their radar
screens. Listening to Wolfgang for the last few days has actually
opened my eyes to things I barely noticed before. Especially the
indulgence in material things which wasn't that apparent in our
parents' generation, certainly not with mine who were both rich
and frugal.

Make a note to write up a proposal for a documentary called
Survival of The Fattest about obesity in American thinking and
lifestyles, based on Wolf's book. Should I ever get back to working
in television. I may be blacklisted for all I know. Certainly no one
except Mike wants to even talk to me. My boss, Al, who I worked
with for years is never available to talk to.

I'd sue them except I'm having to lay low. Whoever is after me
is a real mystery. Why would they want to kill me? I haven't done
anything unless the order from the mob was to kill the entire fam-
ily. I didn't think the Mafia did that. The Colombians maybe, the
Russians, but it was definitely the Italian Mafia that Dad and
Sheffield sent to jail. And why hasn't there been any attempt on
Sheffield? Maybe I'll try and talk to him later too. But for now if
they can't find me maybe they'll give up and go back to New York.

I gave money to Jenny for food and all the booze we'd been
drinking. I've never drunk so much since I was in college. I find it's
very good at keeping me from getting scared and depressed too,
although alcohol is supposed to be a depressant. I'm starting to run
out of money. If I go to my regular bank someone may have put

some trace on my account. Anyway, it leaves a trail. So I'm going to go out of town and hit a series of ATM's. Possibly transfer money into a new account ...

Jenny volunteered to walk by the car to see if anyone was watching it. I told her the make of the car. "I don't know Subaru from a kangaroo. What colour is it?" she asked. So I described it and waited behind a wall while she sashayed by it. She continued to the end of the block, looked in her purse, dug through obviously trying to find something, cursed, then turned around and headed back. I could see most of this from where I had managed to sit up on the wall and could see that no one seemed to notice her. Nor had she. She came up to me and planted a kiss on my cheek. "All clear," she said, chuckling, then waved as she continued in the other direction. "You're not coming for a spin?" I asked.

"No honey, I've got to go to work." She winked then turned the corner. Where does she work? I wondered, before walking down to the car. I hopped in, started the engine, let it idle a bit while I put on the seat belt, then took off. For the next few blocks I turned several different ways, going down side streets and then back onto the main street. Satisfied I wasn't being followed, I relaxed and headed out of town to find a series of ATM machines away from where they were."

It was Wolfgang's turn to relate events. "When you came back to the house I was home fucking the dog. You had some bread, so you offered to take us out for a few beers. We went to the Main Hotel ..."

The Main was a dump on Main Street that only dealers, bikers, drunks and a few radicals like Wolfgang would have the nerve to go to.

"So you think you lost whoever was after you?" asked Wolf after they were served two mugs of beer.

"I didn't see anyone follow, nor did Jenny," he replied.

"Where'd Jenny get to?'

"She went to work." Rory said, still a little bewildered as to where that might be.

"Work?" Wolfgang was also suddenly distracted. "Oh, yeah, I forgot about that." He smiled and quickly changed the subject. "You know why I like it here?"

Rory looked around dubiously, "No idea," he said quite honestly, "Why?"

"There's no rich people, that's why." He saw that Rory didn't quite get the whole idea, which in Wolfgang's mind went back to the Dadaists and Surrealists. "So how long you worked in TV?"

"About ten years."

"You know the media rant on and on about crime, it's just to keep the people scared."

"You're right about that. More and more we're covering sensational murders, sex offenders. Who cares about Michael Jackson? And because of it miss covering the important stories."

"Like how corporations are switching labour to third world countries to make our shoes dirt cheap. The banks are loan sharks, with their compound interest. The stock exchange is a giant roulette wheel, with the banks at the centre as dealers."

Rory gulped his beer. He knew where this was going, and though he thought Wolf could be an amusing guy, he could also be a pain.

"You buy a house and you pay twice as much in interest as you do in principle." Wolfgang went on. "And what does the government do?"

"What?"

"Well, fuck all, besides taking their pound of flesh in taxes. Then they get the poor to waste their little money on lottery tickets."

"I suppose it gives the poor suckers some hope."

"That's exactly what they're giving — hope. They don't want the poor to get better off, because it causes inflation. There'd be a revolution if they didn't keep them all mindless with TV."

"What would you do, ban television?"

"Why not? it can't get any worse. Hey, I got to do something. Can you wait here? I'll be back in the time it takes you to have a beer."

Rory looked up agitated. "Sure. I suppose." He glanced around the place realizing that as soon as Wolfgang left, he'd be out of there as soon as possible.

"Oh, don't worry about anything. They all know me." Wolf said as he got up.

"And that's the last anyone ever saw of you, Rory," said Wolfgang getting up from his seat in the living room. Well, I for one, need a beer. Anyone else?"

Although Rory became much more cheerful over the next couple of days and felt like he was safe at home, his memory still eluded him.

Because he didn't really remember her, and seemed almost timid sexually, Jenny made up a bed for Rory in the small bedroom she'd used for storage, and Wolf and a friend of his carted the stuff she didn't want to the Sally Ann, and the rest was piled into closets or stuffed in the garage at the back.

Each night, though, both of them were woken by Rory's cries from the vivid nightmares he was having that pierced the dark with a jolt of high voltage electricity.

The nightmares were so real to Rory that he believed them — even after he'd woken up. And the following day he'd tell

Jenny or Wolf, or both of them what he remembered. It occurred to Wolf that perhaps they could use his nightmares to unravel his past. But it wasn't that easy. Rory was convinced after one dream that he had killed Suzanne. He saw her on a bed with blood pouring out of a wound, and he with a knife. It took Jenny all morning to convince him that while Suzanne had been killed by a blow to her head, she had not been knifed, there was no bed, and Rory wasn't there, according to reports and witnesses Wolf had accessed. But a doubt remained in Rory's mind. And Rory also knew that he was capable of murder. Still, in a way he was making some progress. Now, at least, he remembered Suzanne. Anyway that was the way Wolf and Jenny thought about it.

Wolf, for all his odd behaviour, attracted people who were invariably overtaken by his enthusiasms and wild, but brilliant schemes. One of whom happened to be a young psychologist. Carl Junger, as Wolf called him, was enticed to come and give his analysis for free. Because none of them knew much about Rory or his circumstances, and Jenny was adamant that they not attract attention or let anyone know his whereabouts, Junger was limited in what he could theorize. Which, he said, made it more interesting.

"I am working from a blank slate," he told the three of them after the initial interview. "Rory," he smiled at him, "has a missing gap in his life of about three weeks?" he turned to Wolf, who nodded. "During that time something happened to erase or block his memory. Correct?" This time he smiled at Jenny.

"So it would seem. He was fine the last time we saw him," said Jenny.

"An accident? A drug overdose? A beating involving head injuries? Or something else," continued the young psychologist who scratched his scraggly goatee. "What do you think, Rory?"

Rory stared at the three of them individually before answering.

"I woke up drunk. Could it be from a drinking binge?"

"Perhaps, but usually the person, while unable to remember what happened during the black-out, remembers who he is, his friends, his work, et cetera. You apparently did not even remember your friends."

"I have vague memories of being in a ... hospital. No, not a hospital — a clinic, or something like that," Rory told them. He hadn't recalled that before so Jenny and Wolf looked at each other with some satisfaction. Rory had a sudden jolt of energy that tore through his entire nervous system. "A prison? Was I in a prison?"

Now everyone was confused. Wolf looked at Junger. "Can we check the hospitals to see if he was there?"

"I'll give you some numbers to call. But a prison? Perhaps he was picked up again."

That idea had a whole new ominous ring for both Wolfgang and Jenny, both of whom hated cops, prisons, courts and authority in general.

"I can find out about that," said Jenny.

"I'm not sure if it was a prison," Rory said shyly, "It just seemed I was restrained. There were bars. But everyone wore white ... I think."

"A loonybin?" Wolf asked before he realized Junger was glaring him.

"I'll check into that," he said. "Loonybin!"

Chapter Six

Rory is watching McElroy and Hudson sitting at a table in an expensive restaurant away from everyone else. Although he is several tables over he can hear them, and for some reason they don't seem to notice him.

"You're quite sure Jesson doesn't know anything?" asks McElroy.

Hudson, who looks much more subservient, and less threatening, looks McElroy in the eye. "Absolutely."

"And nothing was found in the boxes he couriered?"

"Only family photo stuff. No tapes. No files."

"Maybe he doesn't know he knows something."

Hudson briefly smiles, then turns very hard. "That's the only reason he's alive, sir."

"Okay, keep an eye on Jesson, but in the meantime Sheffield is the only other likely person to know where the tapes are."

"Maybe, but the Sheffields hadn't seen the elder Jesson for some time, as you know."

"Check it out anyway."

Rory can't hear that well and moves closer to the table.

"And how far should I go with this?" asks Hudson.

"Be creative. We have to know. We have to get those tapes."

"That's going to require a certain amount of pressure. Sheffield will figure out what all this is about. He'll be a very loose end."

"As I say, be creative. We can wrap both Jesson and Sheffield up in this Mafia revenge business, for example ..."

He lets the implication sink in, as he sips his wine.

"Both of them?"

McElroy looks right into Rory's eyes, then smiles at him. "If you have to."

Hudson lunges at Rory.

Rory woke up. This time Jenny was lying next to him. "Another one?" she asked.

"It wasn't really scary. Just bizarre. Like a surrealist film by someone like Bunuel."

"Okay, honey, who's Bunuel?"

"A Spanish filmmaker. But the people. I recognize the people and they're plotting against me.

"Who are they?"

"I can't," Rory exploded, "fucking remember."

When they all met again two days later none of them had been able to find out anything about where Rory had been. In the meantime, Rory's nightmares had continued. On the night Jenny had come in, she had gently held him until they had started kissing. Good, thought Jenny, This is the Rory I knew. But it wasn't. While half asleep, Rory had a large erection which had been rubbing against Jenny's groin, but when his eyes opened again, and focused on Jenny his hard-on turned to jelly. Jenny had a strange feeling that Rory was deeply embarrassed about something.

"I don't know what's wrong with me," he said in an agonized whisper.

Nor do I, Jenny thought. But she rocked him back to sleep, feeling in a sense closer to Rory because of his vulnerability.

Jenny didn't mention it to Wolf or the psychologist. Rory had become tired and had gone upstairs to lie down. Junger looked worried.

"Unless we know more about him, there's little more I can do right now. There's a mental block, and I suspect it's over a trauma."

"His father died — was murdered — recently," said Jenny.

Junger gave her a rueful look. "Don't you think you should have told me this before?"

Remarkably, Jenny looked embarrassed. "I just thought it was because he was beaten up."

"So tell me everything else you know that might help."

Jenny told him what she knew. Wolfgang added some of his observations.

"So perhaps part of this is just a nervous breakdown from the murders, although it seems to me he's had more trauma than that. Let me make some inquiries. Whatever the case, Rory needs serious help, more than I can probably give. We need to know his personal details."

Jenny was going to object to that, but she also realized how serious Rory's condition was, and instead nodded in agreement.

After Junger had left, Rory came back downstairs. Wolf had gone off to do some work and Jenny and Rory were watching TV — more to avoid talking about the situation than anything else. Rory unconsciously flipped the channel to the one he used to work on. It was an early news show. Rory watched for several minutes, then looked with sudden interest.

"Last night former Secretary of State, Jack Sheffield, and his wife Margaret were murdered at their home in Connecticut. Police are calling the murder a possible Mafia hit in revenge for Sheffield's work in breaking up mob families several years back. This may also be related to a possible murder some weeks back of Victor Jesson. Here's that report," the announcer read.

Jenny too sat up with renewed interest.

"We've suspected for some time that Victor Jesson may have been a Mafia murder in revenge for putting away so many mobsters. Jack Sheffield was also threatened after the convictions ..." On screen was Lt. Freedman. And Rory suddenly stood up.

"I know him," he yelled. "And I know Sheffield ... and Victor Jesson! That's my father!"

It was a breakthrough of sorts.

That night the dreams returned. Rory had gone back to sleeping with Jenny at her insistence. In the first dream he is in his father's house watching two men give his father a needle and start asking him questions about tapes. His father looks distraught, Rory wants to help him, but is afraid of the two large thugs. Hudson appears and starts asking questions to his dad, who is sweating.

"We know you took them, where are they?" demands Hudson in a voice full of pure evil.

Victor looks like he is in great pain, and very weak. "I don't have them," he manages to say.

Hudson leans over Victor's face. "Who does have them then? Your lawyer?"

Victor shakes his head.

"Your son?" Victor's eyes widen. Hudson smiles. "So Rory has the tapes?"

Victor looks terrible, he is trying to say no, but nothing comes out. Rory is on the stairs watching from above, just as he had done as a little kid, when he and his brother had snuck down the stairs to snoop on the adults. Rory looks bewildered and frightened, as they shoot Victor in the mouth at close range. Rory is shocked by all the blood. He screams. Hudson looks upstairs sees Rory and they all start chasing him.

Rory woke up. Jenny was holding him again.

"No! Stop!" Rory said, still half-asleep. Jenny looked at him thinking he was talking to her, but realized he was still in what ever nightmare he had been imprisoned in.

"It's okay. It was just a dream," she said, reminding herself of a mother with a little kid.

After Rory realized where he was, he tried to remember the dream. "A terrible dream. But, you know, it's bringing back some memories. They had my dad ..."

"Who had your dad?"

"I'm not sure, but I recognized one guy ... from the hospital. I was in a hospital ... No, not a real hospital, more like a psychiatric sanitarium. The guy in the dream who was questioning my dad, was questioning me."

"What did they want?"

Rory had to close his eyes to try to remember. "Something to do with tapes. In the dream they wanted to know who he gave 'the tapes' to ... and that's also what the same guy in the hospital wanted from me. I was scared ... in the dream. I couldn't move. I couldn't help my old man. I was frozen."

"It was just a dream."

Rory looked at her frustrated. "No. It was all true. I've been scared all my life. Scared of nuclear war, scared of a police state. Shit I was so scared I'd jump at loud noises."

"Me too, but mine's from smoking too much weed." Jenny

started to laugh, but Rory gave her a frown.

"But I'm not scared any more, and I'm starting to remember things. The dream implied my dad gave me the tapes. But I don't think he did. They've been looking for them ... they've burgled me twice ... the tapes must be somewhere else." Rory was now sitting up and quite lucid. The dream had acted as a catalyst on his memory. He didn't remember a lot, but what he did recall he was certain of.

"Maybe in security locker, or whatever they call them, in a bank?"

"What?" Rory was suddenly lost.

"The tapes. Maybe he put them in a security box?"

"Maybe, but there's something else. He did give me something, but I can't remember what."

"Don't try."

"Don't try?" Rory almost yelled that out.

"If you try to think of something it never comes. It'll pop up later, if you forget about it ..." Jenny smiled gently and leaned over and kissed him. They began to make love, but after a minute of kissing Rory jumped up.

"They brainwashed me."

"What?"

"They had me in a dentist's chair or something. They were trying to fuck up my mind..."

Jenny frowned. He was regressing, which was bad news, and it looked like making love was off the menu, again.

Chapter Seven

Rory had been spending some of his time going through his tapes, and also looking through the files on his computer, which he had no trouble remembering how to do. The computer files were mostly work related, but the tapes were almost exclusively a record of his thoughts after his father had died.

The memory of his father's funeral came back as he listened to what was the first tape.

"As I watched the rain pour down on my father's coffin, I thought I felt a tear run down my cheek, mixing with the rain droplets which were splashing on my head despite the umbrella I was holding up. I was somehow relieved that I still had feelings for my father, however mixed up they were, and that I wasn't another of the mourners who were here out of some obligation.

My father, despite his complexity, was a moral man if judged on his own terms. He had helped shape my character with his insistence on honesty, and had then wondered later, when I became an adult, why I had little tolerance for the kind of duplicity he engaged in on a regular basis. I was wishing that I could have explained that to him, but our communications had consist-

ed mainly of arguments. Being brought up in different eras meant having different philosophies. He was born during the depression, and grew up in war-time Canada. He went through university in the early 1950s, at the same time beginning his climb up the corporate ladder. I grew up during the boom years of the 70s, and never knew what he was really talking about, because he was an autocrat and a company man who saw everything in dollars and cents.

Even the same person would have different philosophies in those different circumstances. I couldn't blame him for that. Although I certainly had done.

The group of twenty or so were gathered around the grave, partially hidden under umbrellas. In better circumstances, and weather, it would have been picturesque. Large willows overlooked the site, manicured bushes and flower gardens ran between the mausoleums and elaborate gravestones. A graveyard of the rich I thought, and looked around at the others, most of whom were executives with McElroy Inc, or old clients of my father. This was what forty years of dedication and loyalty brought. Half aware of what the priest was reading, I peered around at the people looking for familiar faces. They all seemed to be listening to the eulogy, but behind their funereal masks it became clear that they were all thinking of deals they were in the middle of, or things they'd forgotten to do at the office. Only one face, that of Jack Sheffield, seemed sincere. Sheffield was probably my father's only friend.

As I was thinking this he moved forward to read a poem. It was Dylan Thomas' "And Death shall have No Dominion" — a poem my dad would have liked had he ever read it; but Robert Service, his favourite poet, probably the only poet he ever read, wouldn't have been appropriate. Sheffield read it eloquently and with passion.

"Well, rest in peace, now," I said to myself when he'd finished, and the coffin had been lowered in the ground. Peace was something I don't think he ever had. His whole life seemed to me to have been one crusade after another. It's ironic that the old man was basically an atheist, yet led such a puritanical life. He'd never remarried since my mother died. I'm sure he'd never had sex since then either.

I blew my nose with a large Kleenex, and furtively wiped the tears from my face as the ceremony ended, and the "mourners" came towards me to offer their condolences. Conrad McElroy, one of the world's richest men and my father's boss, was the first to shake my hand.

"You've lost a father, and I've lost a man who was almost a brother to me," said the tall, robust seventy-five year old. "Please call me, if I can ever be of help." He gave my hand one last vigorous shake, and moved along, flanked by his flunkies, which included his son, who in childhood had been a close friend. It was apparent in his manner that he no longer considered me such now, although he gave me one of those awkward New England hugs, which ended up as a tap on my shoulder. I nodded and mumbled platitudes to the others who followed, none of whom I really remembered. The last to offer his condolences was Uncle Jack, who stopped, put an arm around my shoulder and gave me a melancholy, yet comforting smile.

"There's some things I want to talk about. Would you be free for dinner in the next day or so?" His grey eyes were slightly moist, making them look unusually serious. I told him I'd like to, and would phone him later.

I watched the expensive cars drive off and walked in the other direction up a path toward a wooded area. There I stopped under a sprawling oak tree, and thought about the meaninglessness of life. A flash of a memory reminded me of a night when my father had talked about having a wake. He'd had a few; a few too many.

I would have liked a wake. But not with these people. I got a sudden shudder, a deep feeling that my father's spirit was lost somewhere. Was that what wakes were for? to give the spirit friendship and courage to find their way to the next world? I didn't even know why I was having these thoughts, I no more believed in an afterlife than he did. I was becoming confused. I could still not believe he was dead, or that he would ever kill himself. Too much a Catholic to do that, no matter how much he said he'd lost his faith. He'd once told me he thought humans were programmed to believe in a god, and I'm sure he never really lost that instinct. The cause of death had been listed as either a suicide or an accidental mishap. And the accident part had only been added at the insistence of his lawyer to prevent any scandal. The cops were certain it was suicide.

Still, I hadn't seen my father for some years. Who knows how lonely he might have become, alone after my mother's death. But Sheffield might know. Uncle Jack, in fact, would be the only one to know. Maybe that's what he wanted to talk about.

Why would my father commit suicide? It had been rattling around my brain since I first heard the news in San Francisco, where I had been covering a political demonstration. On the plane, a couple of hours later, I'd fallen asleep and dreamt of Dad. He looked thirty years younger. Fit, healthy and most of all virile. Very much alive, not like the last time I saw him. In the dream he was trying to tell me something, but as usual I had trouble understanding him. Then it occurred to me he was dead. At that, he started to float away. Singing. It was like a game of charades. Was he trying to tell me something? It felt like I had just glimpsed into the netherworld.

I woke up, greatly surprised to find myself looking down 50,000 feet onto golden fields of what were probably wheat. All I could remember for sure was how well and healthy he looked, and that made me happy.

I drove the rented Sunbird through the winding roads of coastal Connecticut that led to the house I grew up in. Coming into the driveway the old home looked like it hadn't changed at all. Some of the trees were taller, but the house was exactly as I had last seen it fifteen years before.

I took the key my father's lawyer had given me that morning and went in through the thick front door. The carpet was messed up from all the police coming and going, I guess, but the furniture in the living room was the same. Instead of the stereo I remembered there was a modern multi-media centre. Otherwise I might have just stepped back in time. I went through the hallway, past the study and guest room, to the large recreation room we spent most of our time in. It overlooked the ocean, and I passed by the billiard table to look at the view once more.

I immediately regretted never coming back. I'd returned for Christmas the first year after my mother died, but it was such an awkward three days, and Victor, as I called him at the time, was so dismal and uncommunicative that I had made excuses the two other times he had asked me back. I was busy with my career, my new wife, and my friends. But now I felt depressed that I hadn't done more than phone or write once or twice a year.

I drifted back through the rooms and went upstairs looking through the bedrooms trying to decide what I should preserve as family heirlooms and what I should just discard or sell. I wished my brother was here to help decide, but he was in Nepal somewhere and no-one had heard from him for two years. Half of this was his, but I didn't suppose he'd want anything anyway, being a Buddhist who'd already given away all his earthly belongings. I mentally picked out a few old things which I thought had been in the family for a generation or more, then went down to dad's study to leaf through any memorabilia I might want to keep.

I ordered in some Greek food and started through the desk

and cabinets.

By midnight I'd boxed all the photos, personal letters, documents, tapes, CD's and super 8 mm movies dad had shot of all our European vacations. There didn't seem to be much of his business stuff. What there was I put into garbage bags, and went up to my old bedroom. The bed was gone, the room was bare, so I slept in the guest room and dreamt of people from my childhood I hadn't seen in twenty years. Then, as if in a panic, I awoke. There was a figure at the window beckoning me. It looked like a ghost. Then I saw it was my father.

"Dad! Dad! What the..." I started to say.

"Revenge this foul and unnatural murder," I seemed to hear, although his mouth didn't move.

"Murder? They murdered you? Who?"

But my father had gone, his image disappeared. Not like in the movies where it slowly fades away. This was sudden as if he hadn't been there in the first place. And he hadn't. I woke again, finding myself caught in my sheets, struggling. This time I hit my hand on the headboard to make sure I was really awake. I was. My hand was red and it was throbbing with pain. I got up and went downstairs looking for a drink to calm my nerves, and my tape recorder to record the day's events. I usually only did this with work projects, but what had happened today was something supernatural. I wanted it on tape, and decided to keep a record of these strange feelings."

What was it, "foul murder"? No, "foul and unnatural murder." That sounds Shakespearean, he thought as he stopped the tape. Macbeth? Hamlet? One of the great dramas, anyway. He hooked his laptop onto the Internet. Within ten minutes he had the passage from Hamlet Act one Scene 5. He read it and reread it, but he was still no clearer in the meaning of the dream. Rory had read Freud and Jung and some other psychologists, and was looking for some symbolism, but other than the obvious — his father, like Hamlet's, was murdered — there was none; that he could see anyway.

Listening to the tape had brought back a whole slew of memories. And Sheffield. Rory remembered going to see Jack Sheffield and his wife, who were his parent's best friends and like family to him.

He remembered that day. He had packed all the family possessions he wanted to keep and waited until the movers came, then drove around for some time looking for familiar sights from his childhood. First he stopped at the beach where he and friends had spent much of their free time in childhood, swimming, boating, and later, partying. Rory sat on a log smoking cigarettes watching the sea birds, listening to the waves lap the shore, his mind seeing short, jumpy historic super-8 films. He'd given up smoking a couple of years before, but as he began to register the stress he'd accumulated over his father's death, and the nagging feeling that it wasn't a suicide, he had picked up a pack of Camels. And while he felt bad blaming it on Victor, the tobacco did relax him. The beach hadn't changed much, but there weren't nearly as many birds as he remembered as a kid. All the shore birds he never remembered the names of had either died off or gone away and all that remained were the seagulls he'd never liked much. The scavengers.

About three o'clock he drove back around the area filling his mind with memories of what he supposed was a happy childhood: rafting down the river, the fishing holes, trees he and his buddies had climbed, romantic parking spots ... he stopped at some of these places for a time, until he realized it was time he should head over to the Sheffield's.

Rory parked outside Jack Sheffield's house. It hadn't

changed either since the last time the Jessons were there as a family in the 1980s. Back then, he recalled as he walked towards the house, they'd sailed on Uncle Jack's yacht with his teenage children, and got pissed a lot with the older folks, arguing about politics, religion and US foreign policy.

Rory went around to the back of the house to see the huge lawn where they used to play football, badminton and baseball all those years ago. The edges of the garden were covered with rambling native wild plants that gave the property both privacy and a sense of neatly unkempt wilderness all the way down on both sides to the cliff overhanging the Atlantic. It began to rain, which gave the place a haunting feel. He went back to the front door and rang the doorbell.

Margaret Sheffield answered the door, and impulsively gave him a hug.

"I'm sorry, Rory, I didn't attend Victor's funeral. I've never liked funerals. The next one I go to will be my own, or possibly Jack's ... whichever comes first. At our age," she stopped while ushering him into the living room, "each day is precious."
Rory started the recorder again.

"I forget exactly everything we talked about at the Sheffields. Jack filled me in on all the sailing adventures he'd been on since retiring. The first year both of them had sailed through the Panama canal and spent a year dropping in at Tahiti, Fiji, Samoa, Tonga and Brisbane. My dad had been invited but he'd made a number of excuses. Looking back I wish he'd have gone. I mentioned that.

Coffee and liqueur followed dinner as we became like the extended family I'd remembered. At about ten o'clock Margaret excused herself and went upstairs. Jack got up and stared out the window. I sipped my drink.

After a while I asked him when he had last seen Victor.

Jack seemed reluctant to discuss this and began pacing along the terrace window, looking up at me, then away, avoiding steady eye contact. Then he told me that they hadn't seen each other much for some years. Hardly at all since my mother died. Victor seemed to have become a bit of a recluse, especially since he retired. They saw him for the odd dinner, but it was a rare occasion. He really changed in the last five years, Jack had said.

"Enough to commit suicide?" I asked rashly.

Jack turned and looked at me, his eyes harsh and surprised by my question, but gradually dissolving to a look of compassion. "No, I didn't think so." He sat down.

So I asked, looking into his blue-grey eyes, hoping to find truth in a man I'd known and respected since I was a kid, if he thought it could be murder.

Jack poured each of us a couple of ounces of Drambuie, before replying, something like, "If anyone murdered him, and I can't for the life of me believe he'd kill himself, it would be the Costacapas. You know, the Mafia family that he worked on with me in the 1980s."

I was stunned. I had known almost nothing about that episode in my father's life. In fact, I was beginning to realize I hadn't really known my father at all.

Jack went on, telling me that Victor was the brains behind finding all their assets and proposing legislation that took those assets away from criminals, and had got rid of one whole Mafia family, and put others on the run. All their ill-earned gains went back to the state. "There were rumours that there was a contract on me and Victor," Jack concluded.

"But that was decades ago."

And he hadn't had any further threats. Nor had my father that Jack knew of. He looked at the table again.

"Still, Victor was a fighter, he proved that in the Korean War, and I don't believe it was in his nature to kill himself. Especially like that," Jack had said.

I hadn't known anything about that either, except that he joined up in Canada.

Then Jack lay another big surprise on me. "Victor worked for Canadian intelligence."

I wasn't expecting this at all. So Jack elaborated telling me how he had ended up with a lot of CIA contacts, which was why he moved to the States after the war, and went to Harvard. The contacts had helped get him in there, he wouldn't have got in otherwise.

Jack shrugged, and I could see that he was getting tired and the conversation was bringing back his unwanted memories too.

"I appreciate your candour," I remember saying, and left shortly after, thanking Jack for his and Margaret's hospitality.

I got out of the driveway then decided I'd had too much to drink, parked the car on the shoulder and walked home. It had stopped raining, all was very quiet and I was able to think quite clearly about what I had just heard, but not really digested.

When I got outside my house, I noticed it was very dark. I thought I'd left a light on. As I opened the front door and flicked on the light switch nothing happened. I felt through the house looking for the fuse box, but I never got that far. I remember seeing a flashlight, getting scared and then being hit over the head from behind. I passed out for some time. When I did get up, my head was aching like there was a siren blasting through it. And when I finally got a shot of whiskey in me I noticed the house had been burglarized; everything was in shambles. The media centre was gone, and who knows what else. I dialed 911.

The local police came in about five minutes, and we went through the house, me telling the two officers what had disappeared. I noted that the study had been gone over, but wasn't sure *if anything was missing, and the files I had put in boxes earlier were scattered over the kitchen floor. The only items I could recall for sure were the sound system and TV centre, which I had intended to sell, or give away anyway.*

They made notes, radioed into headquarters and left about midnight, telling me that there had been a rash of B & E's of late."

Rory stopped the recorder, thought to himself what it all meant, then went out for a walk to clear his mind. Some of it made sense, and some of it he remembered now. He definitely remembered his childhood, and it was a very privileged one far and away from Mafia and hit men. It made no sense.

Chapter Eight

Rory walked through the east-side streets without any particular destination. That is, until he saw the Main Hotel. That apparently was the last place he had been seen. Did he have the nerve to go in and see if he could remember something?

Rory's first answer to himself was, No way. But as he stood there looking at the place, and remembering the last time he was there with Wolfgang he changed his mind.

He tried to be as non-threatening as possible, yet not look scared, which is always a tall order. He was relieved to see there were not many bikers in that afternoon, and sat down somewhere near to where he and Wolf had sat before. He ordered a pint and sat watching the men playing pool, and occasionally glancing at the TV monitors which were all running some hockey game. A few solitary people were watching, and there were groups of other working types shooting the shit at tables. No one paid much attention to Rory, which suited him fine. Relaxed, he sipped his beer and tried to remember the first time he was in there.

By the end of the first beer he had visualized talking to Wolf, and seeing him leave. Then what? Rory's first reaction was that he probably just got up and left. This was not his sort of bar. He ordered another beer and stared at the door. There was something significant there. He remembered watching Wolfgang go out and almost immediately a beautiful woman had come in.

That couldn't be right, he thought. A beautiful babe would never come in here, not the beauty he was seeing — a woman of about thirty wearing an expensive suit. Rory closed his eyes and tried to visualize what had happened. As soon as his eyes closed the entire scene came to him.

Rory remembered being actually a little relieved when Wolfgang left, the guy was getting on his nerves, which were edgy anyway. But as he looked around the bar and saw an enormous biker staring at him he picked up his mug with the intention of downing the rest and fucking off. Just as he was raising the glass to his lips a stunning woman in a tight pink suit came through the front door. Has she ever made a mistake, Rory thought, beer suspended in front of his face. She was blonde, well-built, athletic even, and had the confidence of a lawyer or successful business woman. Rory got up to approach her, as an act of chivalry as much as magnetic attraction. She obviously regretted coming in and looked around anxiously, perhaps for a telephone, but when she saw Rory coming over she gave him a smile of relief.

"Can I help you at all?" Rory asked as he got near enough to smell her expensive perfume. "You look like you maybe came in the wrong place."

The woman gave a sigh of embarrassment. "I'm kind of lost. I'm an American visiting Vancouver, and I came out of Chinatown, and onto ... is it Hastings Street?"

"No, Main. Where are you headed?"

"I'm trying to get back to my hotel."

Rory was edging them back towards the door, before the

giant biker got interested. "Do you have a car?" he asked, then peeked over his shoulder to see what the other patrons were doing, which was mainly staring at the blonde.

"Yes, but I left it at the Four Seasons."

"You are in the wrong side of town. How did you get here?"

"Oh, one of the tourist buses dropped us off in Chinatown. I'm from San Francisco... I wanted to see the differences. Your Chinatown is nicer, but ours .. well ours is bigger."

"Isn't everything in America bigger?" Rory couldn't resist. "You want me to get you a cab?"

"Would you mind." The blonde gave a little shiver. "I was kind of scared out there. I'm Roxanne, by the way."

Rory held out his arm and led her back to the door. "Rory, and it's no problem. I can walk you down the block, we'll be out of the rubby area at least. C'mon."

Rory got up and led her out the door. On the street Henning pulled up to the curb driving a private ambulance. Before Rory could understand what was going on, Roxanne stuck a gun in his back. Rory half-turned to see a completely different Roxanne. Now she looked dangerous, and very much in control.

"Get in the car, Jesson. This is a gun in your back, and I'm an FBI agent."

"T-this is Canada ... you have no jurisdiction." Rory managed to stutter.

"So what? I've got the gun. Get in the car." As she said this she opened the back door and shoved the gun further into Rory's liver area. Rory crawled onto the stretcher and Roxanne slammed the door, walked around to the passenger side and quickly got in the ambulance. If any one did notice, they were too pissed to bother about it.

Henning hit the accelerator. Roxanne leaned over her seat and with a syringe that Rory didn't see until he was stabbed in the arm with it. Rory yelled, went into a convulsion, and soon passed out, falling back on the stretcher.

That's it, Rory said to himself, out loud, as he opened his eyes. He was sure that was what happened. He looked around the bar. Now people were watching him. Time to head off, he thought, as he dropped a tip on the table and made for the side exit.

Back at Jenny's place Rory told his new friends what he remembered. They were pleased to hear he remembered that much, even though it didn't make much sense.

"And what happened then? And why would a beautiful broad go into a dive like The Main?" asked Wolf.

"Maybe she watched you leave and then figured Rory would come to her rescue," said Jenny. They were sitting in the living room sharing a bottle of wine Rory had bought. In his bag had been a cache where he had kept most of the money he had taken out of ATM machines, and he felt a lot better not having to bum off Jenny.

"Or maybe she didn't know what it was like, it doesn't look that bad from outside," said Rory.

"It's Main Street, Rory," said Wolf with a sarcastic look.

"I know, but she said she was American. I'm sure."

Jenny poured more wine into the glasses. "But who was she?"

"Not Mafia, I'm sure of that," said Rory.

Rory took them out for dinner and they spent the evening enjoying themselves at some café Jenny suggested which had live acoustic music.

That night Rory made love to Jenny like he had before his

blackout. At least that's what Jenny felt. Rory instinctively remembered why he was so attracted to her as well. She was probably the best lay he'd ever had. That he could remember at least. They both fell asleep satisfied. Perhaps it was because Rory's mind was relaxed again, and the fear had left him; anyway, although he felt good going to sleep, his nightmares that night were the worst of all. Rory felt that he was awake the whole night, tossing in the bed, and the dreams were so realistic it was like a vision. They vaguely reminded Rory of a Hieronymous Bosch painting — the one where birds were pecking at humans in hell.

When he finally woke up Jenny was holding him. "Another one, hon?" she asked.

"I just don't understand what's going on," he said, his voice cracking.

"Take a break. Try not to dwell on it all for awhile," Jenny suggested.

So for the next two days Rory tried not to think too much about the whole affair. It gave him panic attacks, and brought back an insecurity that only went away when he drank. So he drank. Wolf, who never seemed to have anything much pressing to do, hung out with him, while during the afternoons Jenny went to work.

"What does she do?" asked Rory. He and Wolf were at The Railway Club, a Vancouver pub that had a long history of playing alternative music and supporting lefty causes.

"You don't know?" asked Wolf.

For a minute Rory thought, O my God, she's a hooker. He shook his head, afraid to ask.

"Exotic dancer. That's what she calls it. A stripper, Rory. And one of the best."

"I'd like to see her some time," Rory grinned.

"Don't tell her I told you. She thinks you're special," Wolf shook his head with a big smile. "Can't imagine why." He lifted his glass and they gave each other a toast.

That night in bed Rory was recollecting some vague memories to Jenny.

"I was at some kind of hospital, I must have had an accident," he told her.

"No, it wasn't a hospital. Wolfgang checked them all," Jenny said. "There were people after you. And Wolf and I think they've been fucking up your mind. Why?"

"They were asking me questions. But I don't remember specifics."

"What sort of questions?" Jenny asked, trying to jog his memory.

"My father," Rory finally said after closing his eyes and trying to put himself back there. It was painful. He remembered being in a lot of pain. "Something about my father's death."

"You thought he was murdered."

Rory kept his eyes closed and could see Hudson in front of him asking questions. Hudson looked like Alex Trevek, for some reason. "They think my father gave me something."

"What? Try and remember. We know they're after something."

Chapter Nine

The next morning Junger, Wolfgang, and Jenny were sitting in the living room as Rory came down stairs. He looked tired and depressed. As they'd been discussing him, there was a moment of silence that Rory obviously picked up on.

"Rory I'd like to hypnotize you. See if we can find out what happened," Junger said to Rory. Turning to the others he added. "I think he was in prison, maybe psychologically tortured."

Rory stood nervously, almost like a schoolboy in front of a group of doctors. He seemed unable to look at anyone. He shuffled over to a spare chair and sat down nervously.

"What does it involve?" he finally asked, still not looking at anyone.

"Wait a minute!" Jenny almost shouted. "How safe is this?"

"It's perfectly safe, I've done it several times. Rory, it's just like you see in the movies. I distract your mind and your unconsciousness awakes. You'll feel like you're half-asleep." Junger sounded more confident than he looked, but then he was younger than all of them, except Jenny. Just out of medical school.

Rory managed to look up at Jenny. Then stared at Junger looking for confidence. "I'll try it. I've nothing to lose," he finally realized.

Jenny looked like she thought differently. Wolfgang seemed okay with it. Junger moved his chair in front of Rory and started the process until Rory looked hypnotized. He placed a tape recorder on the table with the microphone aimed at Rory, then asked the first question.

"Rory, two weeks ago you were in some kind of a hospital or prison. Do you remember?"

Rory started to shake. He seemed to have trouble articulating his thoughts, which were all fighting inside his mind. After a moment he calmed down.

"I'm in a cell, but it's all white ..."

Rory described being in a modified cell that was once used for violent psychiatric patients. The ceiling was so low he couldn't stand up straight, and the room so small he couldn't go any further than to the dirty commode provided for toiletries. He was monitored and various audio tapes were played at loud volume to try to influence his unconscious mind. The voices told him that he was weak; a child in a man's body; that he had homosexual tendencies, and other such taunts aimed at weakening his spirit. He was entirely naked, and it was very cold.

When he awoke the first time he was totally confused, and weak, and extremely hungry. He timidly called out for someone to come. For several hours no one did, although Henning and some assistants were viewing him on video in a nearby room. Finally a large-bellied man dressed in drag showed up with a tray, on top of which was some sort of gruel and a glass of water. The man gave Rory some suggestive looks before passing the tray through a slot.

"See you later, gorgeous," he said as he waddled off.

The same happened the next day, and the one after that. The gay man never answered his questions, which were along the lines of, "Why am I here? Where am I? I want a lawyer." Instead the man either laughed or stared at Rory's crotch, or blew him a kiss.

Although the food looked awful, it was quite nutritious and also spiked with a variety of psycho-neurotic drugs, designed to unhinge Rory's sense of reality. Every time he tried to sleep Rory was awakened by electric shocks from the bed, or loud rap music, which played each hour stopping for a few minutes, then starting again. It was the same song over and over, with lyrics that were graphically homosexual and sadistic. Then on the fifth or sixth day, losing sense of time and reality, Rory started trying to pace the tiny cell. He was becoming increasingly uncomfortable and disoriented. He couldn't sit down for very long, because they gave him shocks through the bed. He had to relieve himself in a kid's potty.

He began to yell strange threats. Day by day he looked more depraved. Even the transvestite had trouble flirting with him. Eventually he put the blankets on the floor to avoid the shocks. But as soon as he finally dozed off, the music increased to ear-splitting levels. Then one day, or night, Rory noticed something strange, and it took him some time to realize what it was. Silence. They had stopped playing the music, he could hear nothing, not even the usual sound of electric hum in the background. Not birds singing outside, not the scurry of cockroaches. Just silence. And for several hours it was lovely. In fact he drifted off to sleep for more than the usual half-hour of exhaustion he was used to. And he dreamed. And the dreams were not pleasant. He was running through corridors in some futuristic slum. The claustrophobia was intense and Rory was looking for an exit out into sunlight. Out into anything. The further he went the more lost he realized he was. He had vague memories of the places, and he knew he was going the wrong way. Through one door he was in a party. He recognized some of the people. People he didn't like very much and a lot of people he didn't want to know, who looked like dope fiends. A big fat woman, he recognized as an old next-door neighbour who would have loud parties, accosted him.

"So, you're too good for us?" she said. Rory looked around and noticed that it was his old apartment, and many of his possessions were in it. "These are my things," he told her. She laughed and repeated what he had said to her young partying friends. Rory walked into another room. It was bare except for a large glass of wine which he grabbed and drank. Behind him a woman called him. He turned to see a beautiful, voluptuous twenty year-old with exotic skin. Before long they were making love. As he undressed her, he suddenly needed to pee. He ran out of the room to find a toilet. There was one in the middle of a kitchen. He aimed at the bowl, but missed much of it.

"How come you're pissing on the American flag, Rory?" A voice asked.

Rory woke up to find himself peeing on the floor. On an American flag.

He realized the voice was coming from the speaker. Were they programming his dreams? That was the last thought he had before falling asleep again. This time he was back with the girl. He was driving out in the country. An ex-cop was with them. One that Rory had to interview several times whom he had never trusted. But now the cop was super-friendly. He asked Rory to stop while he went into a court house to fetch something. The girl was still smiling and he kissed her. Looking back through the window he noticed the truck was a lot larger than he first thought. He tried to back it up, then couldn't find the brake. He asked the girl to look behind him, then backed up. They heard an immense roar. Rory leapt out of the cab of the semi-trailer and saw a bear lying under one wheel. A bear with one of its arms completely cut off at an odd angle to the body. His right leg was also amputated and the bear was trying to stand up, but prevented by the trailer which was on top of his other leg. Rory panicked. What could he do? Worse, what would the beautiful babe think? The cop returned, unconcerned. He looked at the bear, said, "He'll be all right," then asked Rory if his father had told him any secrets. How odd Rory thought. Secrets? Why would Dad tell me any secrets? Where was Dad? Then he remembered, and with that memory he awoke, to hear the wall speaker repeat, "What secrets did your father leave you?"

By the time they came for him, Rory was almost shell-shocked, in a comatose state, unshaved, dirty and above all very scared. Two large men grabbed him by both arms. They needn't have bothered being rough because Rory was already subdued and would have put up no fight. They took him down the hall into another cell that had a real bed and a flushing toilet and a TV attached to the ceiling at a height of almost ten feet, although Rory probably didn't notice any of this at the time. The larger man, Gord, grabbed Rory's arms while the other put his wrists into shackles that were attached to a chain that ran to the wall above the bed, allowing Rory to walk from the bed to the can or to the door. He could also move his hands enough to pick up a plate and eat, but only had a stretch of about a foot between his wrists. He was pushed onto the bed, then a nurse came in and gave him an injection in his thigh. It was a large needle and it hurt Rory, but it immediately made him relax, and he curled himself onto the bed and lay down comfortably for the first time in weeks, or however long he had been here.

It was in fact two weeks after being captured by Roxanne Mallory and Dave Henning that Rory was brought into a room strapped to something that looked like it might have once been a chiropractor's chair by Big Gord. Hudson, who had arrived a week earlier, accompanied Henning. They were both dressed as doctors. Hudson, amicably greeted Rory.

"You've been quite sick Rory, how do you feel?"

Rory unexpectedly regained some of his former character. "Why am I here?" he asked. His voice was weak, but there was a resolve that started to worry Hudson. He had purposely been waiting for the right moment to confront Rory. He needed to know what Rory knew about his father's affairs, and he needed a very submissive Rory to do that.

"As I said, you've been sick, not physically," Hudson hesitated to find the precise words, "but when you came here you were maniacal, raving. You'd been sent to us for observation and we had to put you under sedation."

Rory knew there were several things wrong with Hudson's statement, but he didn't know what. So he sensibly asked, "If I'm sick, why are you keeping me in a cell?"

"You were punching and kicking the doctors and nurses, we had to restrain you. And you kept raving about your father."

Rory hadn't really thought about his father since he arrived. Somehow the mention of him brought back a storm of elusive memories. "My father's dead. He was murdered." He said as the memory came to him.

"You said your father was a traitor. Did you know that?" Hudson stared at him with magnetic eyes that made him look very much like a scientist who was brilliant but also a little deranged. But Rory saw a streak of complete ruthlessness in the man and hesitated before replying feebly.

"You're full of shit!"

Hudson gave him a false smile. "We've got all the files. Your father apparently did betray his country."

A day before, Rory would have believed this, would have believed anything he was told. But something had given him back his courage and also his mental senses. "I don't believe that. He worked for the US government, he helped put away organized criminals ... he worked for the US during the Korean war." Then Rory remembered more. "Besides he was Canadian. Which country did he betray?"

Hudson ignored that and continued his interrogation. "I'm going to systematically prove it to you Rory. Your father was selling secrets to Russia from around 1955 to 1990 when he was caught by the CIA." He held up some papers to Rory, waving them in front of his face.

"He was a homosexual and a communist. They go together, don't they Rory? Gays and commies? Are you gay too?" Rory blushed severely and Hudson gave him a secret smile. "Of course you are. I've seen the tapes."

"My father was as straight as an arrow." Rory managed to say.

"Well, of course it is a shock to you, but you'll see. It's in your genes Rory." Rory glared at him but said nothing. Hudson continued. "We think he gave you some government secrets, and we want to find them. Do you know what I'm talking about?" Rory clenched his fists and shook his head. He actually had no idea, but he wouldn't give them the satisfaction of an answer. "Have you done intravenous drugs before?" Hudson continued, pacing in front of Rory.

"Who are you? I don't know what you want, but I don't know anything, except my dad was murdered."

"He was stopped from passing on those secrets. Rory, I know you didn't do anything, but obviously it's on your conscience. You must tell us what you know, and then we can help you."

Rory found he was starting to believe Hudson. Was his father a spy? He never really did believe in US foreign policy. He thought they were exploiting third world countries and supporting vicious dictators. Rory remembered hearing his father say as much back in the 1980s. Finally, confused, embarrassed, irritated, Rory answered. "I don't know anything. I don't even know where I am. Where is this?"

"You're beginning to rave again Rory, you need some medication."

Hudson motioned to Gord and the other mammoth. They came at Rory from opposite sides. While the one held Rory's shoulders and upper arms, Gord tied up Rory's right arm with a rubber hose and stuck a needle into his veins. Blood flowed into the syringe mixing with a drug that contained a nasty mixture of sodium thiopental and methadrine. Gord pushed down on the syringe. Rory's face contorted immediately. The drug seemed to have an instantaneous affect.

Hudson paced around the room, waiting for Rory to completely succumb to the drug.

"Your father was a traitor, you know that, don't you?"

"No. Yes... I don't know."

"Rory, see you answered truthfully. Now tell me, you ever watch Jeopardy?"

Rory was taken aback by the question. "Sometimes. Why?"

"Well, we're going to play a little game of Jeopardy. Imagine me as Alex Trebeck. Okay, I want you to win this Rory.

91

Ready?"

Rory nodded, and immediately started thinking he was on Jeopardy. He noticed a camera in front of him and smiled as the red tally light came on. He turned and saw behind him the Jeopardy set. In front of him, Gord placed a desk with a large flashing button on it.

"Okay." Hudson even looked like Alex Trebeck to Rory and he smiled at him. "First question. Category is 19th century literature. The book is *Crime and Punishment* ... who wrote it?"

"Who is Dostoyevski?"

"Very good, Rory. You can skip the 'who is' part, we just want the answers. This one's a little tougher. Ready?"

Rory nodded, excitedly.

"This book's central character is threatened with his worst fear. What is the book?"

"1984?" said Rory, knowing he was right.

"And what was his greatest fear?' Trebeck asked with a supercilious grin.

"What are rats?" Rory was ecstatic.

"What are rats. Excellent! And what is your greatest fear, Rory?"

Rory suddenly hesitated, part of his mind realized he'd been conned. But he dutifully answered, "Cockroaches."

Hudson looked pleased. He beamed at Rory. "Now Rory, let's change the game, shall we? Imagine you're in room. It's a small room, with no windows, and only one door. You go to the door ... Are you following this, Rory?"

Rory nodded, then he abruptly saw everything from a completely different perspective. He found he had his hands on a door marked Door 3. He was perspiring freely. His heartbeat was accelerated and he felt the rush of fear. Trebeck smiled again. This time with malice.

"You open the door, and it is a closet full of ... cockroaches, and they jump all over you. Up your pants. They jump on your face, and in your hair. They are in your ears and in your mouth ... Now, don't scream Rory, they'll go right down your throat. Do you want me to make them go away? I'll make them go away if you're totally honest with me. Otherwise, they'll all come back."

Rory, under some sort of hypnosis, could see the cockroaches vividly. They were crawling up his naked legs and he was absolutely terrified. He nodded frantically to Hudson as he smacked at the imaginary cockroaches.

"Did your father give you anything to keep for him?" Hudson asked in a very serious tone. A fatherly tone was what Hudson was trying to suggest.

Rory had to think. He wanted to be honest. He wanted the cockroaches gone, and he wanted most of all just to get out of there to see the sun, feel the wind. Run. "No," he finally said, sure of it.

"Was there anything he left in his will, or his belongings that were from the McElroy Corporation?"

"No, not that I saw. Wait, there was some papers I threw out from his house in Connecticut. No, I think they were stolen with the other stuff."

Hudson knew about that, but he went on as if he didn't.

"Rory, you know you have to tell me the truth. Remember the cockroaches."

"I am ... I'm telling you the truth." Rory was frantic. How sincere could he be? He wished he did know something about it, because right now he'd tell him.

Hudson sighed. In his heart he was sure that Rory knew nothing. He'd programmed this whole operation based on many experiments he had done in the prisons of Central

America breaking communist revolutionaries, whom he had to admit were a lot tougher than Rory. Nonetheless he continued. "You're headed to the death chamber, Rory. Do you really want to go there? You really want to lose your soul?" This was one that really worked on Catholics, Hudson recalled, and Rory was at least brought up a Catholic.

"Fuck you!" Rory spat before his mind fogged over and he was trapped in another hallucination. Only to Rory they were extremely real.

He saw a procession of people shuffling in single file along a dingy corridor. Each person was in handcuffs, and leg irons, and periodically prison guards prodded them to keep moving. At the end of a dismal, dingy corridor there was an electric chair where the prisoners were strapped on. A switch was pulled, by a guard in a Nazi-looking uniform, then the bodies went up in smoke. The next one was strapped in, then poof, was gone. Rory moved up the line. He could smell the fried flesh. This was not hell, this was the end of everything. The end of existence. Rory found himself at the head of the line. The woman in front, who reminded Rory of the girl in his dreams, was crying desperately for mercy as the guard strapped her in. Her eyes were frantically fixated on the switch that the guard reached up for. "Please! NO! " she screamed before an instant later she was turned to smoke.

"Next," the guard said grabbing Rory.

Hudson who was grabbing him, moved into Rory's focus. Rory was still strapped to the chiropractor's chair. Hudson leaned over.

"You're a smart boy Rory. You've heard of the Inquisition. You know, it wasn't all racks and thumbscrews. There was a lot of moral persuasion too. A lot of rhetoric about how not believing in the Catholic god meant you went to hell. They actually wanted to save the sinners, Rory. And I want to save you. You have to believe. You want to keep your soul, don't you? Have you ever loved anyone, Rory? That is besides yourself? Love helps. We love you Rory, help us out here. We don't want to hurt you..."

Rory actually wanted to believe him, but the drug had worn off somewhat, and briefly he regained his courage. He tried to sit up but couldn't. "This is hell!" Was all he could manage.

Hudson sighed, and looked over to Henning. "Henning, this isn't working. We'll have to use the old methods. Prepare for plan B."

The other heavy pushed in a trolley of different devices, all looking very surgical. Scalpels, surgical saws and electronic do-dads, including an electronic device that looked like a small dildo, or a bowel stimulator which he picked up. Hudson motioned to Gord.

"We'll have to try the old-fashioned stuff. " He turned to Rory with malice in his eyes. "Y'know why I hate you, Rory? You had every privilege, every chance to be rich and powerful, and you blew it! You threw it all away. "

Gord, the big thug behind Rory, lifted up Rory's naked thighs and inserted the metal stimulator in his rectum. Then he adjusted the chair so that Rory was now at an angle, with his head below and his ankles strapped to the outsides of the reclining apparatus.

"I'm going to ask you these same questions again, only this time it may hurt. Have you ever heard of the talking asshole?"

"*Naked Lunch.*" Rory replied, briefly back in the Jeopardy game.

"Good, you remember your William S. Burroughs, another queer. But at least he wasn't a communist. What I really want is for you to try to remember what your father gave to you."

"He left me some money and the house, that's all I know, all his work papers were stolen."

"Your father was a communist, Rory, a gearbox. Are you a fag Rory?"

"No."

"Well in five minutes you're going to tell me you're queer ... then you're going to tell me where the tapes are."

Hudson switched the remote control and Rory screamed, his whole body in spasms, dribble in the form of spastic bubbles poured out his mouth. The shocks and Hudson's questions continued in a montage of terror, that left Rory in excruciating pain.

"You're a faggot, Rory. Tell me where the fucking tapes are." Hudson was losing patience.

"Stop." Rory gasped. "I don't know where these tapes are. I swear. Okay. I'm a faggot, but I don't know what you're talking about."

Hudson suddenly lost control. After an hour of keeping his emotions in check he realized that Rory really didn't know and that made him angry. Because, if Rory didn't know, who did? He pushed the button again, this time out of anger, then again until eventually Rory collapsed and blacked out. Hudson looked at the others. Even Gord was looking disturbed.

"He obviously doesn't know. We'll have to get rid of him." Hudson addressed this remark to Henning, who had not been enjoying this, and had looked away when Hudson was occupied.

"Maybe your question is not specific enough." Henning suggested. There was no reason to kill Rory he felt.

"What do you suggest?" Hudson said impatiently.

Henning went over to Rory and shook him. Then slapped

him on the face. "Rory, where are the boxes you shipped from Connecticut?"

Rory opened his eyes, still stunned by the drugs, and pain. Henning repeated his question several times. Rory was so weak Henning didn't think he'd survive anyway.

"They're ... they're still in storage at the Express..."

Hudson smiled at Henning giving him a rare compliment. He turned to Rory. "Very good Rory. And do you have a receipt for that?"

"It must be in my wallet." With that Rory collapsed again and Henning directed the huge male nurse to attend to him. Hudson found Rory's wallet and pulled out a receipt. Then he looked at the nurse.

"Will he live?" He didn't want to admit he'd gone too far, but now he bore no anger at Rory.

"We don't have to eliminate him." Henning said, as if reading his thoughts. "We can create amnesia with overdoses of insulin injections. He won't remember any of this."

Hudson wasn't completely convinced and rubbed his beard. "What if he does?"

"He has no credibility left. Everyone thinks he killed his girlfriend. At least give the guy his life. He hasn't really done anything. As you said, he doesn't know anything ..."

Hudson immediately changed his mind about Henning and it showed. "I don't think you've got the necessary jugular mentality for this type of work. But yes, he probably can't do much to us. He doesn't even know who we are. I'll leave it to you. Just make sure he doesn't remember a thing. And get him dead drunk before you take him back."

Henning and Roxanne Mallory took him into Vancouver and dumped him in a small park called Victory Square, where many homeless men sleep during the summer months.

Junger told Rory that he was going to count backwards from five, and then he would awake refreshed, and remember everything clearly.

Rory's eyes opened and he looked around the room, but instead of looking 'refreshed' his eyes betrayed a native panic.

The enormous terror that he had been subjected to came at him like a raging Rocky Mountain rapid. For the first time since he was a child he got down on his knees.

"Our Father, who art in heaven," he began.

Wolf was about to grab him, when Jenny motioned him to leave Rory alone. They listened to him as he recited the Lord's prayer, almost word for word.

Then he appeared to be in discussion with some spirit, or hallucination.

"Who have you loved?" roared a voice only Rory could hear.

Rory blurted out a bunch of names. Each time realizing he did not love them, and changed his choice to another. "I loved Suzanne," he said finally. Only he knew as soon as he had said it that it was a lie. He loved her for sex, but he disliked her lifestyle, and the way she manipulated everyone around her.

"I love Jenny," he said, although he hadn't really seen Jenny, as all Rory saw was the jealous god of the Israelites who was going to exterminate his soul — condemn his soul to nothingness. He would never have lived, if he could not tell Him that he had loved anyone, just someone, in his 35 years on Earth.

When he had finished saying, "Jenny," Rory got up from his knees and sat back on the couch. "I'm dead, man." He looked at the others, but there was still a glaze in his eyes, that was unhuman. "The terror can't touch me." Rory smiled.

For once in his life, Wolf was left speechless.

Chapter Ten

T he breakthrough meant Rory was calm enough to start listening to the tapes again, and Wolfgang went off on another one of his causes. Dr. Carl Junger wanted to see Rory, but he begged off. The next tape in sequence turned out to be about a meeting he'd had with an old friend, Pete Fraser. Rory remembered him well, they had been pals most of their lives. He pressed the play button.

"At about six o'clock I walked through the Media Club in New York. It was a large venue, divided into several separate sections. There was the TV room where reporters were watching CNN, a snooker table room, and a main area which was a regular bar/bistro. The Media Club was where media people from television and newspapers sat around and shot the shit — about media. I spotted Pete at a table in one corner, and went over. He got up and gave me a bear hug. Pete Fraser is a big man, taller than me by a few inches, and a lot heavier. He had been a linebacker, had gone into sports-reporting for the Herald, and then for some reason he'd never really explained had asked his editor to switch him to investigative journalism. He'd been very successful and had been nominated twice for a Pulitzer. Pete was all charm, and that obviously helped him through a lot of doors that are usually closed to snoopy reporters.

The two of us sat down opposite each other and Pete waved a waiter over for some beer. We talked about the usual things old friends do when they haven't seen each other for ten years, and how our families were doing. Pete was still married to the same woman, who was now a doctor. They had a boy and a girl. I told him I'd got divorced. but that Miles visits every summer for a month. "We go camping, canoeing, sailing. All the outside stuff he never gets back east ... he hates it."

Then by the time we ordered dinner, we'd got around to what we were both doing in our various journalistic fields. His sounded more interesting, and I pumped him for information about some of the stories he had covered. I knew he was good at digging up stuff that others couldn't get. Probably his personality.

We sat and chatted over pasta and wine about old times in Darien, where we'd both gone to high school.

Then something he said made me realize he'd always expected me to come back to New York. "Well, I wanted to live in Canada," I explained. "Here I am born a Canadian and I'd never lived there. I picked Vancouver because it's a beautiful locale, plus I liked sailing in Georgia Strait," And more to the point, I'd briefly worked at a big network where everybody was fucking everybody else to get ahead.

"It's better there then?"

"No. But as I say, it's prettier." Pete let out a boisterous chuckle. The waiter arrived and dropped two coffees on the table. Pete glanced up good-naturedly.

"Sorry I didn't make the funeral, I didn't read about it 'till today." Pete grimaced, he never did like dealing with emotional stuff.

I told him a bit about the funeral, and then about my suspicions about father's death. As an investigative journalist Pete was immediately interested and told me he'd have a look into it.

"To tell you the truth, I don't know anything for sure." I finished, "But I'll tell you what I know, and you can do some follow-ups if you like. I think it may have been a mob hit."

"You must be kidding! Why?"

I told him the story I'd heard from Sheffield, my odd meeting with Freedman, who Pete remembered from an earlier investigation, and my own suspicions. Pete's interest grew, and reaffirmed he'd check it out.

"You've got a couple of options, pal. I can do a story on you. The premise is that you don't quite believe what's going on. I'll phone you later for some quotes, if that's okay with you. At this stage that's all I can do, but the other media will probably pick up on it. The only problem with doing it that way is that then whoever did murder your dad will know you're suspicious." Peter gave me a look that suggested this was a little dangerous.

"I can also do some inquiring. I've got contacts at the FBI, for example. Then when I know more, I'll do a story that will have more substance, and it'll also give us time to dig out the truth. Or at least some truth."

I told him to be careful. That I 'd already got my head bashed in, when I disturbed someone breaking into my parent's house. "They made it look like a routine robbery, but why would they take stuff like the old man's files, and his computer, when there was valuable silverware and china in the dining room?"

"Well, you did interrupt them."

"Yeah. Maybe."

When we'd finished, we walked out of the club together. I noticed two men in a black Ford watching us as Pete got in his car, and they followed me as I carefully maneuvered my rented car from the curb, wondering what the alcohol limit was in New York state. Then I put it down to bad nerves and drove slowly home. I was focused on what was ahead, not what might be behind."

Rory stopped the tape. He was disturbed again. It looked like he was responsible for Pete's death too. He started crying, something he didn't remember doing since he was in elementary school. God, he'd known Pete since kindergarten. And Suzanne? He still didn't know much about that except he had nightmares that he may have killed her.

Chapter Eleven

Junger and Wolfgang met at the psychologist's apartment/office two days later.

"I'm getting complete blanks about Rory. Are you sure you have the right name?"

"I'm sure about his name. He interviewed me last year," Wolfgang said. "What do you mean 'blanks'?"

There's no record of him on Medicare ... that's as far as I've got, but it looks like either he's not who he said he was, or ..."

"Or he's become a real non-person," Wolfgang added.

"I wanted to get him in to see a colleague of mine, but without a Medicare card ..."

"That's a fucking crock. I know he worked at CATV television. He'd have Medicare."

"You don't understand. Rory did work there. But apparently he died."

Wolfgang looked shocked. "What?' he said. "When?"

"The day Jenny said she met him."

Usually Jenny was working during the day and Rory found himself increasingly watching a lot of news programs on television. Since he had remembered working in the media he found watching news helped get his memory back, if only about current events, which had also become vague in his mind.

He was watching CNN when his attention was alerted by a face that he knew. A face that he'd also seen recently, but could not remember where. The program was live coverage of a Senate Committee hearing in Washington. The Senate had become concerned by a FCC ruling over a large media conglomerate trying to buy another one — the already huge Time Warner corporation. The person who Rory was interested in was a man named McElroy who was being grilled by the senate committee, some members of which had expressed their fears that this would create a media monopoly. Rory watched fascinated as the cameras went back and forth from the senators to the distinguished elder business leader that he was sure he knew from his youth.

"Your newspapers and TV stations in Canada appear to favour neo-conservative opinion at the expense of all other ideologies," said Senator Whitman, a Democrat, who had a series of questions to ask the entrepreneur.

"I let the editors and TV directors pursue their own policies and don't interfere with the editorial side of the business at all," replied McElroy with a self-confidence that seemed to unnerve the senator.

"But you only hire editors and TV programmers who have similar political views to yourself."

"Not at all," McElroy gave a sincere look to the panel, then turned to his lawyer. The camera switched back to the senator who seemed to be fumbling with his notes.

"Sir, you've been quoted as saying that in your own newspapers," he said, obviously trying to find those quotes.

When the camera cut back to McElroy he appeared to be helping him out by reading from a paper in front of him. "What I said, sir, is that I hire editors that have a firm grasp on economic issues. Quite often on social issues they write editorials that make me cringe. Sir."

Whitman looked rattled, and the camera had closed in for a tighter shot. "Your father was rumoured to have ties to organized crime, and bootlegged whiskey to them during prohibition."

This time it was McElroy who appeared somewhat unprepared as he conferred with his lawyer, whispering.

"With due respect I don't see the relevance. Besides, you said yourself, it's just a rumour," McElroy smiled, but he looked ruffled, as if he had just taken the first real jab of the bout.

Whitman, when the camera finally cut back to him at a new angle looked pleased. "It's relevant because he started your company, and that company was fined three million dollars in 1932 by the US government.

"Mr. Chairman, this is not relevant to this hearing. Can we move on?" That was the lawyer, Rory realized when the camera finally found him. Rory remembered directing these kinds of programs. When was that? His thoughts were interrupted by the chairman of the committee. Again the camera was too slow to get most of his statement.

"Yes, I agree. Please move on Senator," he said.

The camera quickly cut back to Whitman who looked uncomfortable, turning over papers. Rory wondered whether McElroy owned CNN. He couldn't remember. It would explain the slant that the TV director seemed to be taking though.

"Are you friends with Teddy Thompson, who happens to own the biggest cable TV company in Canada and now in the US?" asked Whitman after a pause.

"We're friends," he admitted freely, giving the impression that being friends with someone has no bearing on anything.

"Not partners?" asked Whitman with a metaphorical

upper-cut.

"No friends from Harvard. Roommates if you must know. But without any business affiliations," McElroy paused for effect then looked directly into the camera, which had zoomed in to a close up. "Whatsoever." He gave the same sort of look that Donald Rumsfeld was famous for, Rory thought.

"As Canadians, you realize that you are restricted in owning media companies in the U.S ... under foreign investment laws."

"I've been an American citizen for over 30 years. And I believe Mr. Thompson has too. And my company is an American company, quite separate from the Canadian corporation." It was obvious to Rory that McElroy was winning the contest, if only through endurance, and a helpful director. But then it occurred to him. What exactly is he trying to get away with here? Because he did remember his father telling him years ago how they often hoodwinked governments all over the world to get their way.

"Aren't you also both members of the Brussels Club?" asked Whitman, who appeared to be running out of steam.

"I'm not familiar with the Brussels Club," McElroy gave a disingenuous smile. Even Rory, with his memory in pieces recognized the Brussel Club, even if at the moment he couldn't quite remember the context.

"It's a club of powerful people that apparently you founded years ago that meets to set world economic policy," prompted Whitman, now with a slight edge in tone.

"Senator, that's probably just another unfounded rumour that certain people, mainly left wing people, have spread about me." McElroy looked to his lawyer, and the camera quickly cut away. I wonder why, thought Rory.

Senator Whitman didn't appear to believe him, but after a

quizzical look moved on. "The Secretary of State, and various other White House officials used to work for you."

"They may have worked for companies I'm on the board of but not for McElroy Communications, senator."

"What about Victor Jesson?"

Rory's antenna flew up. He'd recently remembered who his father was, and who he worked for. In fact Rory remembered seeing McElroy at a Christmas party when he was just a kid ...

"Yes Victor did, but he left us years ago. And he recently passed away. We'll miss him." McElroy looked solemn. Whitman looked frustrated, and sat back. Rory stood up.

"You fucking lying bastard!" he said to the TV. Then, surprised at his outburst, sat slowly back down. There was a pause in the proceedings, and Rory could hear microphones being moved, and watched as the director went to a wide shot. A different senator started to speak, but it was unclear who until the director cut to a close-up during the question.

"As to the acquisition of Warner will this not make you the most powerful media owner in the world?" asked Senator Johnston.

McElroy began to laugh. It was an insincere laugh that even the director couldn't change. "No, there's plenty of competition — Sony, Paramount, G.E. ..."

"But none of these companies control the whole system as you would," said Whitman.

"Senator, have faith in the American market place, it always sorts itself out."

Rory found himself more and more irritated by McElroy's insincerity. How could the panel and the audience believe this guy?

"You will own the most powerful media company in the

world and the means to take over the Internet for delivery of your TV programs, information, advertising, news and movies," continued the senator.

"Senator, it's a gamble. I'm taking a huge risk. And no, I — excuse me — we will not be taking over the Internet. On the contrary, there's more competition on the net than anywhere else."

"As we know from every new industry, there is initially many players in the field, as there was say, in the auto industry before General Motors bought them all up. In the computer industry before IBM took over. Mr. McElroy, with your assets — some say you're the richest man in the world — in five years you may be the only server left."

McElroy's laugh came before the audience saw his granite face. "Richest man in the world, that's rich! Taking over the Internet? That's almost as funny, senator," he said, again reminding Rory of Rumsfeld.

The chairman came back on. "Gentlemen, let's keep this civil, after all, McElroy has contributed greatly to this country. I call for a recess. We will reconvene at 2 PM." The program cut to a commercial, ironically of TIME WARNER.

For the first time since he'd returned, Rory decided to tape his thoughts. He listened to the last part of what was on the audio tape first, which also brought back some memories. He was to spend the rest of that day listening to what he had previously recorded, but first he noted his feelings about seeing his father's boss on television.

"Seeing McElroy on TV jogged my memory. He went way back to my childhood, and I had an amazing transformation. Many of my early memories returned instantaneously. Now it was only the recent stuff that was vague — from the time Suzanne was murdered."

Rory stopped the tape, he had been about to say that he still had doubts about whether he had done it, but realized putting that on tape would be incriminating. Instead he listened to the rest of the tapes until Jenny came home. He told her about seeing McElroy, his recovering memory.

At that moment Wolfgang came in the door. He looked worried. Neither of them had ever seen Wolfgang look worried.

"What the hell's up with you?" asked Jenny with surprise.

"Rory has disappeared."

Jenny's expression turned to complete incredibility. "Wolf? He's right there. See?"

"There's no records of him. They have him listed as dead."

"What?" This time it was Rory.

"Carl Junger checked your medical record to see if you were still covered, and it lists you as dead."

"Which means I'm not me," said Rory with a sense of defeat. "If I had've heard that two days ago I would have believed it."

"I may have done too, except I met you before at that protest."

Rory stared questioningly at Wolf for a moment. "Oh, right. I remember that now."

"So what's happening?" asked Jenny.

"Wolf's right, they've disappeared me. I don't exist. So who will believe me?"

Chapter Twelve

Rory found himself in a large ornate room. There were Impressionist paintings on the walls. The beige carpet was luxurious. He looked down to find he wasn't wearing any shoes. Far off by the verandah, which overlooked a tropical bay, he could vaguely see a group of men chatting. As he came silently closer he could see that McElroy was talking with other people he recognized including cable TV magnate, Ted Thompson, and the man he knew as Hudson. There were two other men who said nothing but listened to McElroy.

None of them appeared to notice him as he crept closer. He wanted to hear what they were saying. He got as close as he dared, then hid his body behind a wall curtain.

"It's like Rome, we control the media and give the masses sex, violence, and then they don't even bother to vote," McElroy said, his colleagues chuckled dutifully. "With control of the Internet we can start getting rid of all those annoying political websites that seem ubiquitous."

"Of course, we also need to have the government start censoring it," added Thompson, a tall, skinny man in his seventies. As rich and ruthless as McElroy.

"Of course." McElroy left unsaid that after sexual censorship, the media would inevitably lead to political sentiment against all the radical anti-American web-sites. Besides, with economic control it would be hard for them to get servers to host them.

McElroy turned to Hudson. "You're absolutely sure Jesson doesn't know anything?"

"Absolutely."

"Maybe he doesn't know he knows something." McElroy turned to the others, who snickered at the play on words. Hudson briefly smiled, then turned very hard.

"That's the only reason he's alive."

"And Sheffield?"

Rory had a strange feeling he'd heard this before, like a recurring dream, only it was somewhere else.

"I can assure you Sheffield knew nothing. He watched his poor wife suffer, and would've told us anything to stop her pain."

"Well, we can wrap Jesson up with his father and Sheffield in this Mafia revenge business, after you find the tapes."

McElroy gave another of his enigmatic smiles letting the implication sink in. Then he sipped his wine.

"Yes sir. Although insanity would be just as good."

"Yes. I've been watching those videos of yours. He's half-mad with paranoia." Suddenly McElroy turned. "And Rory, what are you doing hiding behind that curtain? Aren't you too old to be playing hide and seek?" McElroy said with a guffaw that seemed to drown the room with its resonance.

Immediately Rory ran from the room and through the hallways. He could feel rather than see Hudson on his heels. He flew through the front door and hopped over a hedge, running like a deer, he felt, through the shrubbery and onto the immaculately cut lawn. Behind him he could feel Hudson's whole presence, could even smell his breath as he panted behind him like a hound dog.

Then he fell down a gully, rolling down another steep slope that seemed to lead to a cliff. He tried to brake his momentum with his foot, but it only turned him in another direction — directly towards the cliff. He could hear Hudson's laugh as he rolled over the ledge. Looking down he could see the waves crashing on the Atlantic shore. He plunged down head over heel to certain death. And then something really strange happened. Rory suddenly started to fly.

"Of course. I can fly," he said out loud. He looked behind, saw Hudson on the cliff edge, and waved. Then he woke up, and almost immediately recorded everything he could remember of the dream onto his digital recorder.

After a morning of confusion, Rory was going through his note-book looking for phone numbers. He remembered Al, but had a feeling that he wouldn't have anything to do with him. Most of the other numbers were business contacts, a couple of old girl friends, and Mike. He tried to remember Mike. He knew he was a friend. God, did I only have one friend in this city? he asked himself. None of the others he looked at gave him much confidence, or he didn't remember them. He decided to call Mike.

"Rory! Where the hell have you been. We thought you were dead," was the first thing Mike said to him. "Where are you?"

"I'm okay," Rory said. "But who spread the rumour I was dead?"

"Not sure, pal. Al just sent a memo around saying you'd had an accident, and the body had gone back to New York or wherever."

"I'd like to talk to Al," Rory said, getting angry. "Are you working today?"

"No, I'm doing a shoot on Saturday, so I'm off ... can we get together?"

"Yes, I'd like to, where do you live?"

"Rory? You must've been here a hundred times. You're joking, right?"

"No, I did have a sort of accident, and lost much of my memory. It's one reason I want to talk to you."

Mike gave him the address, and Rory made his way over there by taxi. Mike, who he remembered, but didn't really recall their relationship, gave him a big hug as he came in the door. He offered him a drink and they sat down in the living room, which overlooked English Bay and the Pacific Ocean. Rory told him as much as he knew.

"But there's a blank about Suzanne. I can't even remember exactly what she looked like."

"She was a doll, Rory. How could you forget?" Mike said.

Mike was aware of what had happened up until Rory disappeared the day after Suzanne's murder, and he started to relate some things that had occurred. He told him about the argument that he and Suzanne had had over a shoot before Rory returned from New York.

"She was a doll, but even you said at times she was a bitch," Mike said gently, then related what he remembered. "Well, the day before you got back Suzanne was so pissed off at me that she reported me to Al ...

Suzanne Wilson walked briskly down the halls of CATV studios with an arrogant determination, totally ignoring anyone approaching her. She walked straight into news director's Al Davidson's office without knocking. Because the door was glass she could see Al, and he could see her before she burst in. Al, who was in a meeting with Marie Martin, a senior reporter, was obviously annoyed by the abrupt intrusion.

"Al, I just want to let you know Mike screwed up another of my stories," Suzanne said before Al could say anything.

"How'd he do that, Suzanne?" There was a paternalistic, sarcastic tone to his voice. He could see that Suzanne was fuming, and trying to keep her mental lid on before the steam erupted and blew it all off. Al knew it was a stress-filled job, and he made some allowances for that, but some of these petty squabbles were too much for him.

"He missed the most important sound bite of the whole speech." She told him.

"That's not like Mike ... but I'll have a word with him ..." Al hoped that she'd take her cue and leave.

"Cover it in a voice-over, Suzanne. It's not that important," Marie said with a hint of patronage, and a pinch of rivalry.

Al was now looking at Marie with amusement. But Suzanne was glaring at her.

"Really? Oh, and Marie? That interview you did with Sarah McLachlan? I was supposed do it. I set it up!"

Suzanne turned and stomped out. Marie looked at Al, who shook his head, then shrugged. "What is it about reporters that makes them such a pain in the butt?"

Marie smiled. "Beats me." They both chuckled, and Suzanne could hear laughter following her down the hallway. Another crimson wave seemed to rush up and over her face. She changed direction and headed outside knowing she should cool off.

As Suzanne was walking out in the parking lot, Rory Jesson was thousands of feet above her flying in from Toronto via New York. He was reading the New York Herald. He stopped when he saw his father's photo with a piece by Peter Fraser that gave the highlights of Victor Jesson's career and work with government. He also briefly mentioned the link with organized crime, and the threats the Mafia don made after he was convicted under Victor's special New York legislation. Pete ended the piece wondering if perhaps there were a link to the Mafia with Victor's "untimely death".

He didn't mention suicide at least, Rory thought as he put the paper down and looked out the Air Canada jet's port hole. Down below he could see the lights of Grouse Mountain ski area above the bright glow of the city of Vancouver. God, it's getting big, he thought. Maybe time to move to a smaller place. Victoria? Maybe Kelowna.

After breezing through customs Rory grabbed a cab, and headed across the bridge and down Granville Street to his home in False Creek.

Rory opened the door to his townhouse and yelled, "Suzanne? Anyone home?" Upstairs he could hear the sound of Suzanne's feet running over the floor and down the stairs. She had a huge smile, her white teeth gleaming, and when she got to the bottom she ran over to hug Rory.

"Welcome home!" Rory held her, then pushed her gently back and looked at her. She was wearing a sexy dress that distracted him. As usual, he thought.

"It's good to see you." He said instead, as cheerful as his tired body would allow. "I need to soak in the hot tub. You into it?" She laughed. They kissed again. Then after Rory put his suitcase in the bedroom and his carry-all bag in the study, they both stripped and slunk into the hot tub on his balcony which overlooked Vancouver's harbour area, with a view of the inlet of Georgia Strait and the Pacific Ocean. After they had soaked in silence for awhile Suzanne looked up at Rory.

"So tell me all about New York!"

"I was only in New York a couple of hours. Met a friend."

"An old girl friend, right Rory?"

"No an old boy friend." Rory turned to give her a dirty look, but she was smiling.

"An old boy ... friend?" They both laughed, and brushed each other. It was times like these when he felt he loved Suzanne, Rory thought.

"Yeah, his name's Pete Fraser, he's going to follow up on what happened to my dad."

"You know, you've been doing investigative reporting so long you think everything's a bloody conspiracy. And speaking of conspiracies, can you believe what Mike did while you were gone?"

"No, what did Mike do?"

"He fucked up another one of my shoots."

Rory looked disturbed, but finally said, "You know Mike's one of the best cameramen around ..."

"Can't you at least talk to him?"

"I'll talk to him."

Rory suddenly realized why in the end he had an ambivalent feeling about Suzanne. She was gorgeous, sexy, but she was so ambitious. Was she just using him? he thought. Then again ... Rory grabbed her and started necking with her, and feeling her hot breasts.

"Tomorrow!" he said between kisses.

That morning Rory woke up early, still on eastern time. He slipped out of bed, made some coffee, transferred some files onto his home computer from his laptop, and left for the station before Suzanne had really woken up. He'd kissed her, whispered, "Goodbye" to which she'd muttered, "I love you," then rolled over. Rory spent the early hours in an editing bay looking through footage of a documentary he'd been directing. At about nine o'clock the door opened and Mike MacKinnon walked in. Mike and Rory had worked together for several years doing news stories and documentaries.

"How was the Big Apple?" asked Mike sitting in an adjacent chair.

"As rotten as ever. 'Course, I only spent an hour or so there at the Media Club." He was going to continue the pleasantries, but decided to get the shitty stuff over with. "What's going on between you and Suzanne?" he asked, sympathetically.

"She's been on to you already?" Mike sighed, and looked out the window into the main studio. Rory stopped the item he was working on, which freeze-framed in pause, then turned to face Mike directly.

"Look, I realize you two have what? Personality conflicts? Okay, let's hear what happened."

"She's blaming me for missing a key sound bite. But Rory, she didn't even show up until half-way through the speech. How was I to know what she wanted?"

"Mike, you're not only a good cameraman, you know when to shoot a good sound bite too." Rory's gaze penetrated into Mike's eyes, questioning. He believed Mike more than Suzanne, but still, Suzanne was his lover.

"Rory, I was looking out for her when it happened. Nothing personal ... but she always blames someone else for her fuck-ups."

At that moment the phone rang. Mike picked it up and passed it to Rory. "It's for you."

"Hello?" Rory held the phone at an angle, as the cord was stretched to its limit.

"Mr. Jesson, your shipment has arrived from Connecticut, where shall we send it on to?" Rory looked confused for a moment.

"Oh. Thanks. Can you store it for me?" He hung up the phone after an affirmative answer and turned his eyes back to Mike.

"You just don't like these new reporters."

"Neither do you. None of them, and you know it, have any journalistic sense at all." By this time Mike was up on his feet. "It's all acting now."

Mike looked frustrated and lost for words. Rory tapped him lightly on the shoulder, as he got up, motioning him to follow. They walked into the control room, Rory carrying a video disc to drop off there. They looked through into the studio as the anchorman was doing several takes for a simple promo for the midday news.

"Coming up at twelve, Prime Minister abuses ..." the anchor was reading from the teleprompter. The director in the control room pushed buttons on the intercom system. Rory and Mike and everyone else in the control room could hear the director yell, "Jesus Christ! He can't even read properly... idiot!" The floor director in the studio could also hear her, and he smirked; but the anchor, on a separate system could not hear a word of it, and looked up innocently towards the control room. The director flipped another button.

"That's *accuses,* Bob." She paused to control her voice. "Let's try it again. One more time."

"Sorry Jane. My mind's somewhere else today," the anchor whined. He straightened his expensive tie and stared at the camera. The director switched off the anchor's headset again.

"Sure Bob. Maybe if you didn't hang one on every night .... Oh, Why do we have to work with these moroons!" the director slammed her hand on a near-by table. "All right, let's take it again."

Rory and Mike grinned at each other as they exited the

control room. Walking down the corridor Rory turned to his friend, "Yeah, on-air people! Why do you think I try to spend most of my time doing these so-called documentaries?"

"But I'm not so lucky," Mike said. "You don't have to deal with the pretty faces wanting more reaction shots. Acting like they're movie stars."

"I know what you're saying, Mike, but there's nothing I can do anyway. Talk to the assignment editor and see if you can change reporters."

"What difference will it make, they're all the fucking same, except Robert and Trina. If you feel the same way, why don't you and me start our own production company?" Mike stopped in the corridor, but Rory continued walking.

"We've talked about that, you'd just want to do slick looking TV commercials." He smiled as he said that, opened the door to let some young interns pass by.

"Keep this between you and me, okay?" Rory said when they were out of earshot. "But I couldn't work with Suzanne either. I'm not sure I can even live with her."

"Why'd you move in with her then?"

Rory stopped in the middle of the hall outside reception, and looked at Mike seriously. "You got me. I guess I got lonely. She came at me so fast, I felt like I was in a tornado. I mean a great tornado, by the way. When the wind stopped, we were living together." He shrugged, and was turning to leave.

"I'll talk to Karen about reassigning you two. But try and put up with it, buddy."

"Sorry about your old man." Mike said as they both went separate ways.

"That's from what I saw, and from what you told me," Mike said to Rory, as he finished the story. He got up and grabbed a couple more beers from the fridge, handing one to Rory and opening the other with a quick twist. "Later that day the news came out that Suzanne had been killed. I wasn't there, but the first to hear about it was Freda, who went into the news meeting to tell Al …

A group of men and women were seated in CATV's boardroom. This was the daily news meeting where the news director and the various producers got together to assign stories and get an idea how the stories coming in for the day would rate in importance. This time the station manager, Liz Proctor, was also present. As Al Davidson was getting started there was a knock at the door and a young female receptionist stepped in nervously.

"Yes Freda, what is it? We're in the middle of a meeting," said Liz brusquely.

"Sorry to disturb … but I thought you'd want to know. Rory Jesson's just been arrested." Freda replied nervously, suddenly wondering whether it was important enough after all.

There was a silence in the room while everyone looked up at her. Liz broke the spell. "What an earth for?"

"Suzanne Wilson was murdered." Freda blurted out.

"When? When did this happen?" Al piped up.

Freda turned from Liz to Al. "This morning, I think, and the cops just took Rory into custody."

"Thanks Freda, thanks for letting us know." Liz's tone gave Freda the cue to leave and she closed the door quietly as she left. Liz turned to the others, who all looked pretty stunned. "What do we do about this?"

"We run it, before the other stations do." Marie Martin put in.

"Hey, we owe it to Rory to find out if it's true, don't you

think?" Al was on his feet, and looked around the table as he said that.

"I'll check it out. But if it's true, we got to run it." Dave Lui was a young up-and-coming producer, who treated Al as his mentor. "Don't you think, Al?" he added carefully.

Liz, who was getting a little impatient at all this democracy got up. "It's your call, Al. Meanwhile, I better make some phone calls." She walked quickly to the door, turned to say something, thought better of it, and shut the door. Al remained standing and turned back to the producers and reporters at the table. His face betrayed a certain quandary that was going on in his head. "It doesn't sound like Rory. Maybe the cops are just checking him for motives."

"Maybe," Marie replied, "but Suzanne and Rory were fighting a lot. She told me. And he has a temper. We've all seen that at times."

"That's going back a bit Marie ..." Al gave her a look. To the others he put on his professional face. "Okay, Dave you check it out. Keep it quiet; if he's innocent it'll ruin his career. Marie, you write an obituary on Suzanne, find some good intros and stories she's done. We'll run that for sure. Get a crew over to her house."

"She lived with Rory." Marie said quieter than usual.

"All right, his house. I want it on the 6 o'clock."

At about the same time Rory was sitting in a holding room in the Vancouver Police Station. The only other time he'd been in a jail was when as a teenager he and some friends (*Was Pete there?* he wondered) had been busted for smoking pot. That time had been a bit of a joke as they were all stoned. This time he was alone and nervous as hell. They'd told him Suzanne had been killed when they picked him up. One of them had asked,

"When was the last time you saw Suzanne Wilson?" He told them, then asked why. They'd asked him if he could come to the station. Again he'd asked why. This time they told him. At the station he'd been offered the chance to speak to a lawyer, but had naively refused, thinking it may make them think he was guilty. He was beginning to regret that. For more than an hour he had watched hardened criminals being taken past his room — it wasn't quite a cell, but it felt like one — some of whom stared at him with malice, and others he got the even worse impression they were looking at him as a prospect for sexual abuse.

Finally, the two cops who'd brought him here reappeared. They'd been back to the crime scene, then had taken a coffee break to make Rory sweat a bit. Neither of them had much use for media people. Without much decorum Rory was led through the hallways by the two homicide detectives, Leonard Chan in front and Eddie Marshall behind him, who guided Rory into an interview room where they offered him a seat. Marshall, the senior of the two, remained standing, and began the interrogation.

"Because you lived with Ms. Wilson, you are at this time a suspect in her murder. However, you haven't been charged, and you have the right to a lawyer, and the right to remain silent. Do you understand?"

Rory, who was still shaken by the news of Suzanne's death nodded distractedly.

"Did anyone see you leave for work?"

Rory sat back in his chair and tried to think. "Yes, the lady across the hall was picking up her paper when I left at eight o'clock. We said hello. Then I got to work at about 8:20 or so. They'll have a record of that. We all have to sign in."

"And Suzanne Wilson was asleep when you left?" Marshall

continued.

"Not asleep. But she was still in bed."

"You've had fights with her before?" This was Chan, who was standing behind Marshall. Chan's voice had a mean edge, that Marshall's lacked. Good cop, bad cop, Rory thought, before answering.

"The usual. Jealous spats, I suppose. She had a temper, and was pretty upset I didn't call her much when I was in New York for a week."

"When was that?" Chan again.

"I just got back yesterday. I was there for my father's funeral." Marshall held his hand up behind his back so that Chan could see, "I'm sorry to hear that. But, we did hear that you and Ms. Wilson had, uh, volatile ... quarrels."

"Who said that?"

"Your alibi for this morning. She does say she saw you at eight or so, and then heard some yelling afterwards. If your office confirms you were there by 8:30, you're probably telling the truth." Marshall signalled Chan again, and he made to leave the room.

"Of course I'm telling the truth,," said Rory angrily. "She may have got on my nerves at times, but I'd hardly kill her." Chan stopped at the door and stared at Rory.

"Any ideas who might have wanted to?" Rory noticed the pleasant tone of Marshall's voice, and relaxed somewhat.

"No. But maybe her ex. Pick one! I don't know. She was pretty vicious when she got mad."

"You don't seem very upset about her death." Chan gave him a wry, almost sadistic smile.

"For Chrissake's. Of course I'm upset. You know, since I heard about it, from you by the way, I've been in your goddamn custody as a ... suspect, you call it. When I get out of here, then

I'll probably start to grieve. If that's what you mean."

Chan ignored that, nodded to Marshall and walked out of the room. He began watching through the observation window outside. A black woman police officer approached him with a fax.

"Did you get a confirmation?" Chan asked her, in a remarkably pleasant voice.

"Yes, reception has him signed in at 8.25. He never left. This is a photocopy of the sign-in sheet." Constable Gerard gave him the sheet, then looked in through the window. "That's him is it?" Chan nodded and started to read the sheet, as Gerard walked back down the hallway.

"Was anything stolen?" Rory asked Marshall just as the door opened and Chan reentered the room.

"Maybe you can tell us." Marshall said after reading the report Chan handed him. "Your story checks out. Care to come and look over your place with us? Until we get confirmation of the time of death, you are technically still a suspect, but we aren't going to arrest you, and you are free to go."

Rory, who was beginning to think this might have something to do with his father's murder agreed to go with them. He followed the detectives to his condominium in False Creek. The whole building had been sealed off, and police officers were keeping the curious at bay. Rory walked through the lobby with Marshall and Chan. Outside his door were more yellow ribbons. Marshall motioned for Rory to stop at the entrance.

"You can peek in," he said, "but don't cross the tape, they're still collecting evidence." Rory looked through the doorway. Inside were several officials in white smocks dusting for fingerprints, looking for any clues. "What a mess!" he said under his breath. His eyes stopped at the fireplace. The outline of Suzanne's body lay on the floor, her head at a strange angle on the bricks. "God. Poor Suzanne." Rory felt suddenly sick and stood back, breathing heavily to get air in his lungs trying to avoid the nausea he felt coming.

"Don't go in yet," said Chan. "See if you can tell us if anything's different or missing." Rory held onto the door frame and looked in again.

"It's hard to tell. I don't really have any valuables here, nor did she ... the iMac's about the only thing worth stealing, and it's still here. Wait a minute, did your guys turn it off?"

"No, everything's as it was except they're dusting for prints and other evidence. It was off when we got here, wasn't it Len?" Marshall looked at Chan who nodded in affirmation.

"Well, I always leave it on." Rory said with conviction. "On 'sleep' mode."

Marshall called to one of the investigators in the living room. "Brad, did you turn off the computer? There's usually a little white light under the screen."

"No." Brad went over to the work station. "You want me to turn it on?"

He was talking to Marshall, but Rory answered. "Sure. The switch is on the back of the screen."

Brad, who was wearing latex gloves, carefully pushed the on button. The screen came to life, but after a minute of electronic activity there wasn't anything on the screen except a bunch of odd symbols.

"It looks like the hard drive's been erased. Someone's been in there." Brad pushed a few keys, but nothing came up.

Rory worst suspicions had been confirmed and he now felt greatly responsible for Suzanne's horrible death. He turned and faced Marshall. "You know, detective, I got robbed in New York just a few days ago. Someone's looking for something. As I told you earlier, I think my father was murdered." Marshall listened, but Rory got the feeling he wasn't taking it too seriously. "If you want to talk to someone in New York, I'll give you Lieutenant Freedman's number. He's in Darien, Connecticut." Rory searched his wallet for the number, which Marshall wrote down.

"You're free to go." He said when he'd finished. "You'll probably have to find somewhere to stay tonight. And, keep in touch. And stay in town." He didn't add that Rory was still a suspect, but Rory seemed to get the message. "You may be some help later on. If you think of anything, call me." He held out his card.

Rory took the detective's card and walked away without saying a thing. He glanced at his watch. It was after four. He drove slowly through the city thinking of Suzanne and wondering where to spend the night. He went almost completely through downtown before he realized he was in a trance. Through the car windows the people on the sidewalks looked like they were extras in a movie. He had been infatuated with Suzanne. She was an extraordinarily good-looking woman, belonging to a class — models, film stars and beautiful people — whom Rory had never had much time for, but couldn't help envying. She was smart, but superficial; she attended all the right parties and cultural events, but knew relatively little about literature, art or theatre. She belonged to the new bourgeoisie, who congratulated each other on their appearance, and success, and were more class-conscious than the real aristocracy. In that sense he had disliked her. But besides the great sex, there was a vulnerability he detected in her that drew him to her.

He stopped for a red light, and looked over to the street corner. He saw two hookers waving at him, his face flushed, and he immediately wondered where he was. Was he dreaming? A car horn behind him shook him. He looked up at a dazzling green traffic light, took his foot off the brake, and depressed the accelerator. A sudden eruption of guilt slapped him inside his head. It was his fault they'd killed Suzanne. She had nothing to do with whatever was going on. Rory could barely drive, but was able to pull the car into a parking lot. He found himself near Sunset Beach in the West End, got out of the car and walked to the water. He sat on a bench. It wasn't cold but he was shivering, and put his arms around his chest clasping his shoulders tightly. A faint ringing reached his ears, becoming louder with each pulse. It took several of them before he realized it was his cell phone.

"Hello?" he said woodenly.

"It's Mike, Rory. How're you doing?"

"Terrible. Poor Suzanne."

"Where are you, buddy?"

Rory looked around. "Down at the beach. Near English Bay."

"Listen, why don't you come over here. You can crash on the couch. Maybe a few drinks might help."

Rory had been vaguely thinking of taking a hotel room, but Mike's offer sounded much better. He needed to talk to somebody, and Mike was just the person.

"I appreciate that Mike. I think I'll take you up on that."

"Shoot on over."

By the time he arrived at Mike's immaculate pad, Rory had his emotions more under control, but he was subdued and Mike sat him down and made a couple of steak sandwiches to go with the beer he opened almost immediately. They talked about what had happened, Mike being slightly evasive about what was going on at the station, saying that he had been out shooting all day and, "Thank God I didn't have to cover your story." When the news came on the television, Rory saw his anchorman and reached for the remote to turn up the volume.

"Freelance producer Rory Jesson was taken into custody today after his live-in partner and CATV news reporter, Suzanne Wilson, was murdered in her apartment," the announcer read in a clipped tone. "For that story ... Marie Martin."

"Thank you, Bob ..." Rory silenced her with the remote and turned to Mike.

"Freelance! I've been there over five years! So they all think I'm guilty. It figures, they're all tight-assed ..." He was too frustrated to finish the sentence. He turned the remote back on and they listened to the rest of the story. It mentioned that the police had released him, and at the time there were no suspects, but after the short tribute to Suzanne, before throwing back to the anchor, Marie added that Rory had been cautioned not to leave the city.

"What the hell is that!" Rory stood up, yelling now. "She was never much of a journalist, but that's fucking innuendo. Where'd she get that anyway?"

Mike shook his head, he obviously had no idea, although Rory did — the cops.

Rory wanted to phone Al immediately, but Mike calmed him down and told him to "sleep on it," that he would be calmer in the morning. "I know how you feel, man. Don't let it get to you." Mike was trying to be helpful and Rory realized that and sat down. "Look, I gotta check my mail, see if Pete got back to me. Do you mind? This has all got to do with my father..."

"They'd come all the way up here, you think?" Mike looked doubtful.

"I don't know. They're after something my dad had. Some evidence maybe ... against one of the Mafia bosses." He let it hang, realizing it was pretty vague.

Rory plugged his computer into Mike's phone line then bent down at his lap-top to access any e-mail He glanced through it and stopped on a message from Pete. He read it aloud to Mike.

"It's from Pete: Talked to various sources: Attorney General, FBI, DEA, and didn't get anywhere. The gun was bought at Turnbulls, by Victor Jesson. I'll go there and show him a photo to positively ID your dad. Another guy I know maybe has something. I'm seeing him tonight and will call or e-mail tomorrow."

Rory looked up from the screen and gave Mike a wry smile. "If only the cops were as interested."

"Why's this guy so helpful?"

"He's an old friend. Grew up together. We went through journalism school together, only I ended up in TV. He's good, if there's something funny he'll find it. Just a minute, I'll mail him back."

He typed on the keyboards: "Thanks Pete. Good idea. Get a photo from the obituary on Victor and check that he really bought gun. I don't want to sound paranoid but they're after me for something Dad had. Someone just killed my girlfriend. Another break-in. Take real good care."

"What did you say?" Mike asked, curious.

Rory told him.

"You know what? I'm beginning to believe you."

Rory was sitting on the couch staring at Mike. Some of Mike's story was familiar, other parts of it he either didn't know or couldn't remember.

"You stayed at my place the night she was murdered," Mike continued, "then went to the station to pick up your shit. Then completely disappeared," said Mike concluding the account.

It was beginning to make more sense now, thought Rory, and told Mike his suspicions.

"I hate to tell you this, pal, but most of the people at the station still think you killed Suzanne." Mike saw his friend's expression change to anger. "I know better, but these people we work with are mostly idiots. They're completely caught up in their own shallow little dreams ...."

"I know. I remember now. That's why you were my only friend there. Thanks Mike. I've gotta go. I still want to find out who killed Suzanne. And my dad for that matter."

"Let me know if I can help," Mike offered.

Rory smiled grimly. No, there had been too many of his close associates killed already.

The taxi ride back jogged his memory some more and he recalled driving to the station that morning in a furious mood.

He'd spent the whole night on Mike's couch tossing and rolling. When he did sleep the dreams were of work, and he was behind on a deadline, or he was somehow doing an entry level job and worse, was not very good at it. He got little sleep and was just as agitated when he called the station after a coffee, about 9 AM.

He got hold of his boss, Al, easy enough, but there was a definite coldness, a hesitancy on Al's part to say very much.

"Look, Al, I'm not even a suspect in this, you can't fire me."

"You're not fired. Suspended. At this time, with pay." He paused, and finally said: "Look. It's not my decision Rory."

"I thought we were friends, Al."

"I've got to go," Al said and hung up.

He got much of the same from another "old friend." Other than Mike he was considered a leper at the station. The English had a word for it, Coventry. When they send people to Coventry no one talks to them. In Canada it's "Got to go." Which in a way Rory hated more, because it's condescending as well.

Well, if they wouldn't talk to him on the phone, he'd see them in person.

An hour later Rory was at the front desk of the CATV station signing in when a security guard came towards him.

"I'm sorry Mr. Jesson, you're not allowed in the building at present." The man was intentionally blocking his way. A security guard who was usually extremely obsequious with Rory.

"Why is that?" Rory asked, with both confusion and some animosity.

"Orders from the management. Until Ms. Wilson's murder is cleared up."

"Look Bill, I've already been cleared by the cops."

"I'm sorry sir. I can go and get your personal belongings ..."

"Forget it."

Rory turned and stormed out of the building and into the parking lot without thinking where or what he was doing. He should phone Al, he thought, and clear this up. He gave a scornful look at the TV station as he got into his car putting his bag on the front seat next to him.

Rory paid the taxi and walked a block back to Jenny's house. He was still looking everywhere for tails, for people following him. He'd thanked Mike for the information, but hadn't given his address, because he didn't want Mike to come to any harm. He was beginning to think that he should get away from Jenny's place too.

Unless, maybe they're not after me anymore, he thought as he opened the door. There was no one home, so he took out his tape recorder and noted everything he'd learned from Mike. Then he added a little description of Wolfgang, remembering the day before.

"*Wolfgang is probably the most bizarre and at the same time loving man I have ever met. He does the strangest things. When he needs money he goes downtown in a wheelchair with a patch over one eye and panhandles. He makes a fortune. He's basically a crook. Yet for some reason he's risked possible danger to help me, but that is just part of his nature. I've been reading his book and making notes for a possible documentary, but seeing as I'm officially dead I may have trouble getting the financing.*

Yesterday Wolf dragged me along on another of his completely outlandish projects. I needed a change so I went along with it. First he borrowed a small school bus from a friend at the local community centre. Then we drove down to skid road and picked up as many panhandlers as we could fit in, which was about twenty, and then we drove off to the ritziest, most expensive shopping neighbourhood in West Vancouver and proceeded to drop them off to panhandle the rich.

What of course happened was that the shoppers started complaining to the merchants who complained to the police who came down in several cop cars to investigate. But Wolf had read up on his municipal by-laws and West Van had none that prohibited pan-handling, so while the cops stuck around and watched the hobos continue to work the street, and eventually made quite a bit of loot, as some merchants paid them to leave, and some shoppers, who had never before been accosted by bums felt some sympathy and laid $5 and $10s on our unlikely heroes.

I found myself enjoying every minute and wished I had a camera to videotape the prank. But while we were waiting in the bus for the men to come back I noticed a woman in a car parked two spaces behind. She looked familiar and I stared at her hoping something would click and I'd remember who she was. She wasn't giving me a very good feeling though, in fact I quickly developed a stomach ache from the anxiety I was feeling.

I mentioned this to Wolf, and he suggested I go right up to her and ask who she was. With a great deal of trepidation I followed his advice, but as I got down from the bus, the woman saw me and immediately pulled her car out into traffic. But as she was forced to drive right by me I got a very good look at her. And froze. I had seen her several times. The last time in some dream-like scene in an alley. The first time when she had put a gun in my back and kidnapped me.

I'm sitting here back at Jenny's and now one more clue to this nightmare is before me. But I still can't remember what the hell it is these people want, except some tapes. What tapes?"

Chapter Thirteen

Rory and Wolfgang were having a discussion, or to be more exact Wolf was extolling on the effects of globalization on culture.

"... where before you had people who would sing together, and dance with each other in groups; where people had real discussions; listened to good music like Duke Ellington, and read books. Instead we've got an artificial society where everyone lives with strangers, do little together and complain about their taxes..."

"Or globalization," added Rory, who was beginning to get his sense of humour back.

"Granted," said Wolf grinning. Even if Wolfgang was an ideologue, at least he didn't take himself too seriously.

The doorbell rang. Wolf, peeked outside through the curtain. "It's no one I know."

"I'll get it," said Rory, not thinking about his situation. He opened the door to find a man in a cheap blue suit with a tie that was so ugly it could only have been a present from a visually challenged person. Next to him was a young woman, who might have been attractive except that she wore a dress that was not only out-of-date by a couple of decades, but somehow ratty.

The kind of clothes that are only available at a thrift store. She had no make-up on and her eyes wouldn't make contact with Rory as he looked them both over.

"How are you today, sir?" asked the man.

"Fine, what's up?" asked Rory already suspecting they were Salvation Army or Jehovah's Witnesses. The man held out two small newspapers, the top one Rory could see was called Awake. He tried to remember which cult they belonged to and was staring at the cover when a strange feeling overcame him. He looked at the faces of the two again and knew that he had met them before.

"Not interested," he managed to say, and closed the door. He was having trouble breathing. He couldn't remember the man still, but the woman was definitely the one who had kidnapped him at the Main Hotel.

"Wolf, sneak a look at them again," he said, still breathing heavily as if he'd climbed a steep hill. Wolfgang peeked through the curtain again.

"Who are they?" he asked.

"The woman, I'm sure that was the woman who kidnapped me. They're both part of it."

Wolf didn't need to be told what of. He watched them walk down the street. They acted like they were real Jehovah's Witnesses and knocked on another door. Wolf went to his room and came back with a camera. It had a telephoto lens. He went outside and snapped some shots from behind a pillar on the porch.

When they'd gone Wolf took Rory and the roll down to a one-hour photo shop. They went for a coffee and snack while they waited. Wolfgang could see that Rory was very nervous.

"What did these people do to you?" he asked, but then remembered stories under the hypnosis. "You think these are the same people?"

Wolf considered it some sort of a miracle that the photos from the One-hour Photo were ready in an hour.

"What will they think of next?" he said to Rory as they walked up the street. Back at Jenny's place they went through the photos.

"This is the guy that was following you," said Wolfgang. "He looks different, but the face is the same. And — guess what? — the shoes."

"So we know it's them?" Rory wasn't all that sure.

"I guess so. If it's the same girl. I'm sure this asshole was following you the day I found you panhandling."

The incident of the two probable CIA operatives having the audacity to come to the door scared the shit out of Rory and he became paralyzed once again. Even Wolfgang, usually the man with a cool head, was confused as to what to do. First, Rory wanted to leave immediately, but it quickly occurred to him he had nowhere to go. Nowhere that was safe anyway. Obviously they wanted to let Rory know that they knew where he was.

"But why?" asked Jenny when she came home an hour or so later.

No one had a good answer. The most likely scenario would be to keep them under furtive surveillance. It didn't make sense for them to let them know they were probably being watched.

"Unless they want to spook us," suggested Wolfgang. Jenny laughed at the pun. Rory looked at her angrily.

"Get it? Spooks spooking us... oh never mind," she said. Finally Rory gave a brief smile. But his stomach was churning with anxiety. He was in fact getting panic attacks and was looking out the window every five minutes or less.

"Sit still, for Chrissakes, Rory," Jenny said after a while,

"You're driving me dizzy."

Rory sat down, but was up again in a minute. "Is there somewhere we can go?" he asked.

"An idea," said Wolfgang. "We'll go to one of our clubs. That way we'll be able to see them if they follow. We know everyone there."

Rory took his backpack and they left the house walking around aimlessly, then hopped on a skytrain for a few stops, then back one stop. From there they made their way to a little club that Wolfgang frequented. It was obvious no one had followed them, and as they were going in the door Wolfgang said so. Rory, already paranoid, asked him.

"What about satellite?"

"There's an idea," said Wolfgang sardonically. But it was obvious he hadn't discounted that possibility. "If it's CIA who knows? The NSA can do impossible shit."

Henning looked up from the TV screen with a big smile at Roxanne.

"He's right about that of course."

"How can satellite cameras get so close?" asked Roxanne looking back at the monitor.

"Beats me," said Henning, already preoccupied with the computer switcher. "Watch this! Look at that TV over there." He pointed to a television in the living room. Roxanne turned towards it. Suddenly the program that had been on — a political debate of some kind — disappeared and the image of Rory, Wolfgang and Jenny walking down a street in the east side popped on. Roxanne literally gasped.

"How the hell did you do that?"

"Jamming. I jammed into the local cable TV program." Henning gave her one of his smirks, which always made her feel dirty and disgusted. Henning switched the program back.

"I'm going to make titles, and tonight, or tomorrow, or whenever they get back home — they're going to become the latest reality show. We've got techies already wiring the house with hidden mikes and cameras."

Even though he was still smirking, Roxanne had to laugh. "That's actually very funny, but how the hell will that help us?"

Henning just shrugged — it was obviously Hudson's idea — and got back to making titles on the computer. He typed in a few words. "How about 'East Side Story'?"

This time Roxanne shrugged, then left the room. Boys and techie toys, she thought to herself. She needed a good long shower. She really wasn't happy with this assignment, despite the laughs. She had no idea what they had done to Rory, and she didn't want to know, but he was obviously changed. Not nearly the confident guy she'd first met. She went in her bedroom and started to take off her clothes. Then stopped. She checked the room for hidden cameras.

When they entered the club Rory felt a sense of relief. He wasn't sure why, as he didn't like these clubs much — too many poseurs. Jenny led them to a table in a secluded area where they could watch the dance floor, but were far enough away from the hip hop music to hear themselves.

Rory wanted to leave Vancouver, but he had no idea where. The others weren't keen on leaving their home, and suggested alternatives.

"I've got a friend who'll let you stay there, Rory," said Jenny hopefully. But Rory didn't want to involve anyone else, and that also meant Mike, who he figured was his only other friend in the city. There was something he kept trying to remember. A house somewhere. Not a house, but ... he could see water and trees, and a terrace.

"Jesus!' he said.

"What's up?" asked Jenny.

"There's a place that keeps flashing in my mind. An old memory. But it won't come out."

Wolf pulled out a joint. "Here, try this."

Rory just looked at it and frowned. Pot always made him lose his memory.

"There's always the other alternative."

"What's that Wolf?" Jenny perked up. If Wolfgang was weird, he was also real smart.

"The other alternative is to do nothing." Wolfgang paused and looked at Rory. "Assuming they know we know they're watching, then they'll be surprised if we show up again. They must want us to go somewhere. Whatever it is they think Rory has, then they're probably just waiting for him to lead them to it. We'll play with them, and watch them follow."

Jenny thought that was a great plan. She loved theatrics. Rory didn't like it all, but he was running out of options. The only other thing he could think of was going back to Connecticut and piecing things back together.

Chapter Fourteen

S o for the next two weeks they spent a lot of time going places to see if they were followed. They rarely were. Rory managed to move his car to a safe place close by in case he had to get away suddenly. Wolfgang brought back his doctor friend, Carl Junger.

The first visit was uncomfortable. As Wolfgang, Jenny and Rory sat in the living room, Junger announced that he had tried to find records of Rory in the US.

"You existed all right, but there's nothing there after you came to Canada. Can you try and remember back to when you arrived here?"

Rory recalled much of that quite easily. Driving across the prairies. Staying in a motel in Medicine Hat, where he felt he had mistakenly crossed the border back into the USA with all the cowboys, ranchers and 'You betchas' around the whole of southern Alberta.

He remembered driving through all the small towns in the interior of British Columbia, usually smelling the sulphur of the mill miles before he'd drive through the town. Then he related his first impression of Vancouver.

"Compared to anywhere I'd lived before it was absolutely

beautiful. I'd been here before as a kid, but not since..."

"You came here as a kid? When?" Junger asked.

Rory stopped to think. "It seems we had a cottage, or stayed in a cabin. I remember the ocean, beaches, and it was so different than Connecticut. But I don't remember Vancouver much..."

"Tell us about the cottage." Junger somehow felt this was important.

"Yes, Rory. You mentioned that before," Jenny said.

"It's kind of like a dream now. I remember a small cottage. Primitive. Me and my brother slept in a loft, and above was just the wood of the roof. We'd hear my parents and some friends talking and telling jokes and we'd .... this is funny — the next morning at breakfast we'd tell those jokes back to Mom and Dad." Jenny laughed and Wolf howled.

"You don't remember where it was do you?" asked Wolf, when he'd finished his hoot.

"On an island, I think. Why? Is it important?"

"It sounds like that place you were trying to remember the other day..." said Jenny.

Henning was chuckling as he watched the whole thing live from his studio across the street. He turned to Roxanne who was lounging on the sofa in the living room.

"This is going to be a terrific episode. I won't have to edit a thing."

Roxanne gave him a wan smile and went back to reading her book. She was getting tired of this whole facade. Henning, she felt, was a frustrated film director and had been editing each day's events down to a half-hour show which he jammed onto the TV station. Each day he'd enlarge his audience. How, Roxanne didn't have a clue, but from 7 PM each day 'East Side

Story' would hit the air in east Vancouver for a half hour as the latest soap opera. It must be getting an audience, she thought, because although she hated to admit it Henning was quite good at finding the dramatic moments in the day and editing them — and these often included scenes with Rory and Jenny half-naked, or making love.

"Does Hudson know you're doing this?"

"Of course he does. It was partly his idea," said Henning. "Shh! this is good."

Completely his idea, thought Roxanne. But why was the CIA doing this to Rory? Why were they even in Canada? A supposedly friendly ally. Right now though she was more concerned that this TV show of Henning's might become a cult hit. When would the e-mails and calls start pouring in?

A cult hit! Rory woke from his dream entangled in the sheet. The first thing he did when he realized he was awake was search the room for hidden cameras. After checking the ceiling, the lamp, the curtains, the track lighting he couldn't find a thing, although one of the bulbs in the track lighting wasn't working.

Where was Jenny? He couldn't remember if she'd gone out. What time was it? He wandered into the kitchen to check the read-out on the microwave — about the only clock in the house. It was almost noon. He'd slept a long time. When did he go to bed? Rory couldn't really remember. The last image he could recall was at that club.

Then it came to him. The dream. The dream was telling him about the cottage. The rest of it, the TV surveillance, the club, was all due to anxiety. It was then he remembered the cottage. Back when he was a kid his dad used to take the family to B.C. to visit his folks. They'd spend two weeks at Grandad's cabin. They had to take a ferry to get there. A ferry!

Suddenly Rory smiled. A real wide smile for the first time since his dad died. Then he started to think about the will. At the time he hadn't paid much attention. As his brother had joined a Buddhist cult, Rory'd got most of Victor's assets — the house, and a good deal of stocks and bonds. But there was something else too. Something that wasn't left in the will but had already been transferred to him.

He looked around the house for cameras, before peering through the living room curtains to look outside for any surveillance. He didn't see Henning, even if he had've been there.

When Jenny and Wolfgang arrived back Rory immediately told them he wanted to take them for lunch, still paranoid there may be microphones or other surveillance somewhere. Over Chinese food in one of those restaurants only Chinese eat at he told them about the cottage.

"Where is it?" asked Jenny.

"On an island," said Rory.

Wolfgang looked at Jenny with his eyebrow raised, then at Rory.

"There's hundreds of islands just in Georgia Strait, Rory."

"Yeah, but I found the title to the place. It's on a place called Gambier."

"That's not too far," said Wolfgang. "In fact we could get there in a few hours."

"No, I'll go alone. I'm sure they're watching us."

Rory and Jenny were sitting on one side of the booth, which hadn't changed much since the fifties. Wolfgang took up most of the other side.

"I have to go on my own. Too many friends have died," said Rory.

"That's okay, pal, we ain't your friends."

Jenny tried to kick Wolfgang under the table.

"You're never going to find the place without me, y'know," she said to Rory. "You haven't been to the island since you were a little brat. Hey, Wolf, we'll stop for supplies, then we're headed to ... where is it?"

"Gambier Island," said Rory. He'd checked through his documents earlier and found the deed and a key to the place in his bag in the hidden file section.

"We'd better watch out for any surveillance," said Wolfgang, lowering his voice to a whisper. "We'll split up. They'll follow Rory, if they're watching. So Jenny, you head for Rory's car and pick us up at Lost Lagoon. We'll get supplies later."

It seemed like a plan to all of them. Not a great plan, but a plan, and all of them by now had caught Rory's paranoia, as if it were some virulent flu.

Rory paid the bill, and they all left the Chinese diner in different directions. As far as Rory could tell no one was following them, but with satellite surveillance who the hell knew anymore?

Wolfgang took a bus to Stanley Park, while Rory hailed a cab and circled through downtown telling the cab driver he was American and looking for a friend. Every so often he'd tell the cab driver to turn at random, and checked the rear to see who followed. After a while he got bored with it. No one seemed to be following, so he told the driver to head for Stanley Park.

Wolf was sitting on a park bench when Rory's taxi pulled up. Wolf got up and the two of them started jogging around Lost Lagoon.

On the other side of the bird sanctuary they came to Second Beach, where Wolf ordered some coffees. They stood outside slurping coffee watching for Jenny to drive through the park, and looking for any surveillance.

Rory spotted her first, it was his car she was driving, and the two threw their empty cups in the garbage and ran up to the curb at just about the same time as she pulled up. They both hopped in and they took off to the nearest exit. So far no one was following any of them.

"This is where the high tech surveillance could be kicking in though," noted Wolfgang, looking up in the sky.

"Fuck all we can do about that," said Jenny as she tried to edge the car into traffic on Georgia Street. She was headed towards downtown.

"Hey, where you going? I thought we were going to the ferry," said Wolf from the back seat.

"Relax, Wolfie, we are." Just then she turned left into a hotel driveway, did a U turn and got back on Georgia Street headed for the Lion's Gate bridge, which would eventually take them to the upper levels highway and then to the ferries.

"You probably lost the satellite camera too," said Rory with a grin. They'd made it. Now all they had to do was get to Gambier, then find the cottage. Then?

Chapter Fifteen

Outside on the top ferry deck Rory, Jenny and Wolfgang were sitting in the evening sun watching the scenery. Wolfgang had everyone's attention.

"Mankind consists of two very different races, the rich and the poor," he said philosophically.

"That's real profound Wolfgang. You make that up?" asked Jenny.

"Nah, that was Louis-Ferdinand Celine. A Frenchman."

Rory, who was wearing sunglasses against the glare from the sun, and had been looking at the scenery, turned to Wolfgang.

"Celine wrote 'Journey to the End of the Night?"

"I certainly didn't write it. But I am doing a Sci Fi about aliens who come down here to eat all the fat slobs in North America. They conquer us easily, by offering free beer which makes them all zombies, then they line up all the fat people like cattle and have a big barbeque ..." Wolfgang increased his volume with the last sentence.

Rory and Jenny didn't have to look to realize that some of the other passengers were quite obese. Both had to stop themselves from bursting out laughing. Jenny, who was clutching her stomach trying not to laugh, motioned Wolfgang to shut up, then gave him a kick.

"Shut the fuck up!" Rory whispered. But Wolfgang wasn't finished.

"It's not funny. Look around, how can all these fat slobs be poor?"

"Maybe they're well-off, Wolfgang. Shut up already." Jenny said through clenched teeth.

"Nah, the rich take their own boats or fly. These slobs eat too much junk food and watch too much junk television. Fast food people are fat food people who also like fast fat cultural junk, seeing and hearing the same fucking things over and over and over," said Wolf."

"Wolfgang!" Rory said quietly, "There's lots of slim people. Look at her." He pointed to a slim woman reading a magazine. "Hey, she looks familiar." Rory stopped. He knew where he'd seen her. The Jehovah's witness. "Let's go below," he said to the others, his paranoia evident in his voice.

When they arrived at a ferry terminal named Langdale they found they would either have to wait for the small Gambier ferry or they could drive into Gibsons and hire a water taxi. They opted for Gibsons and the water taxi, mainly because Rory was so agitated about being followed.

Rory, who was now driving, parked the car away from the dock, hidden from view from any road. They walked down through the old section of Gibsons and stopped at a store to buy some more groceries. By now Rory had relaxed as there had been no signs of being followed. They went down to the dock and hired the water-taxi to get them to the island.

Wolfgang and the boat's driver, Roger, hit it off immediately. Jenny sat back and watched the spectacular scenery. Rory spent a lot of the trip looking up at the sky and behind in the boat's wake. There was no one following, but about half-way to the island a helicopter flew over the top of Keats Island and then towards them. Rory started to duck to hide from them, until he realized how dumb that would look.

"What's that helicopter?" He asked Roger.

Roger just shrugged, and laughed.

"It's probably Search and Rescue," said Jenny.

"Nah, they're bigger and orange," said Roger, grinning. "You should see the mothers they use to find Grow Ops — black as night."

Rory watched it fly overhead nervously. He tried to see if they were looking down at him, but he couldn't tell at all.

On Gambier, they asked directions of a tall, wiry man with long grey hair and a beard. He told them it was about a mile walk along the road, and then down to the shore. As usual Wolfgang became instant friends with the man, and by the time they started their hike, he had laid a quarter ounce of 'Gambier Gold' on Wolf.

About an hour or so later they found the cottage. It wasn't quite how Rory had remembered it, but the key he'd been given with the deed worked, "So this must be it," he said.

"Too bad we didn't bring any beer," said Jenny.

"I got a sack of wine instead. Easier to carry in," said Wolf smiling and pulling a square box out of a backpack and placed it on the driftwood coffee table.

"Is that all you brought?" asked Jenny.

Wolf dumped out the rest of the stuff from his bag. "No, I bought food too." A pile of packages of dried pasta, dried rice and beans, dried peas and dried sauces hit the table.

"Wolf, baby, we're not camping. Thank God I bought that Barbie chicken."

Rory looked around the place, then climbed the ladder to the loft. Wolf literally crashed on the old futon couch, while Jenny went to the kitchen for some glasses.

"Yeah, this is it. I remember the loft," said Rory as he came back to the living room area.

"Nice place," said Jenny as she poured three glasses of Okanagan wine out of the four litre case.

"Yeah nice pad, man," said Wolf with his usual sardonic tone. "Quite the view."

A balcony the length of the living room looked out towards Howe Sound to the Coast mountains which jutted straight up from the ocean to the snow-covered peaks eight thousand or so feet up. They gave a sense of a great era which preceded the age of humans. Below them lay a sandy beach with large driftwood logs that the tide had swept in many years before.

Rory raised his glass in a toast. "To good friends and happy memories."

"Memories anyway. I'm glad you got yours back," said Jenny. "Salud. This is God's country."

"God? what do we need a father figure for?" Wolfgang was up to his usual mind games.

"It's an expression ... like ... this is heaven ..."

"What's the point in an afterlife if we don't live this one?" asked Wolfgang.

Jenny threw a pillow at him. "You're hopeless. A hopeless atheist."

"So you're not afraid of dying, Wolfgang?" asked Rory, still obviously nervous.

"Of course I'm afraid. There may be a few old friends

who'll miss me, but I'm really going to miss myself the most."

Jenny laughed and threw the other pillow.

That evening they ate the barbeque chicken with rice and peas. After which Rory and Jenny went upstairs to the loft to bed, and Wolf lay down on the futon couch under a sleeping bag.

Outside a full moon rose over the mountain peaks and a long ray of slivering light reflected on the wavy water. It was deadly quiet. So silent that for sometime Wolfgang didn't understand why he couldn't sleep. He was so used to the city traffic sounds. In the loft Jenny and Rory had no intention of sleeping, and eventually the rocking of their lovemaking seemed to soothe Wolfgang enough at least for his brain to call, Lights out.

Rory had not made love like this since before the torture sessions. It had taken him some time to overcome the psychological fear that had made him impotent for the first couple of weeks on returning. Now he remembered why he felt such passion for Jenny. Her body and his worked so well together. Just when he thought he would burst, her body would relax and so would his. Long deep kisses would bring them close again to orgasm, till finally they both climaxed waking up Wolfgang momentarily and probably the family of Steller jays that nested in the nearby bushes.

Rory soon fell into a deep, contented sleep.

Rory entered a large mansion. It reminded him of Xanadu, the palace from Citizen Kane (and Kubla Khan), except this was in bright, rich colours. He'd been here before, but couldn't remember when. He heard voices, but couldn't see anyone at all. He was now in a huge room with thirty foot ceilings. He recognized some paintings. A Renoir. One of his favourites, the one with all the umbrellas. The little smiling girl. What a sweet smile, but the more he looked, the more he wondered — her eyes were the eyes of a mature woman. And a Manet? He felt he could almost walk into it. There were a small group of people lounging on the grass at a picnic. Two men, fully dressed, appeared to be discussing something, and a naked woman sitting next to them was staring right at him.

"What are you staring at?"

For a moment Rory was stunned. It was a man's voice. Yet he didn't see any lips move.

"Do you like my paintings, Rory?" This time the voice came from behind. Rory turned.

Conrad McElroy was standing there, his face muscles smiling, but his eyes cold as icicles. "I'm sorry it has to come to this."

"Come to what?"

"If you give my people the tapes, we'll leave you alone. On the condition you don't listen to them."

McElroy seemed to be much taller than he was the last time Rory had seen him. Or at least Rory, who remembered being about the same height, felt smaller. Maybe he should just give him the tapes. Only he didn't know where they were.

"I have no idea what you're talking about ..." he almost added 'uncle' which is what he remembered calling him when he was a child. "Your good Uncle Conrad," his dad would call him.

McElroy walked away. In the background Rory could see a group of people seated on the verandah. He saw Hudson get up and walk toward McElroy, who gestured behind him towards Rory. Hudson walked quickly and methodically towards Rory like a military man on a mission. Rory turned and fled. Before he could change course he ran right into Boccioni's *The Mother*. It was the most terrifying painting Rory had ever seen. Inside it was far worse. He ran under the clenched fists, and tried to hide under what at first appeared to be a dress, but turned into a dark tunnel full of a gangrene coloured blood. He turned right, but smashed into a brick wall. His body felt elongated. He found he could twist around. His whole body was as flat as a pane of glass, then it shattered into pieces like stained glass. He tried to put himself back together, but the pieces kept changing. He couldn't walk, because his legs were where his arms should have been, and finally he couldn't find his eyes, and even if he could, his hands were missing ...

"MOTHER," he cried. "Mom, help!"

"Rory, wake up!" Jenny was shaking him. Rory's eyes opened.

"Thank God, I can see."

"Another dream?" Jenny frowned.

"It's morning?" Rory could see daylight through the skylight. "I'm going for a walk. That dream was terrifying. Bizarre, but ... I'll tell you about it when I get back."

Rory walked along the shore for some time completely lost in thoughts. What was so scary was not the painting so much as McElroy. He knew McElroy was behind this all, and he was one of the most powerful men in the world. Perhaps he should just call it quits and move to Australia or somewhere away from his grasp. And he also felt an obligation to Jenny, and to Wolfgang. They'd looked the night before for any sign of tapes, but found nothing. There was not much in the cottage anyway. The storage shed just had gardening stuff, and the boat shed had a fourteen foot row boat, an engine that probably needed a good tune-up, some gas cans and an old canoe.

There were a few boxes in closets, and coats and stuff which were covered in plastic. After a couple of hours of aimless walking he returned to the cabin to the smell of coffee and frying bacon.

"Wolf at least remembered to bring coffee," Jenny said as he came through the door. Wolfgang was awake but still laying on the couch.

"We're going back," Rory announced.

Jenny turned from the wood stove with a jerk. "What? We just got here."

"Let's at least look some more for the tapes," said Wolfgang.

"No. I keep having these dreams. They're like premonitions. The one last night McElroy told me not to listen to the tapes ..."

"McElroy?" Wolf yelped. "That son-of-a-fuck. If he's behind this then let's bring the fucker down."

"To tell you the truth, he scares the shit out of me." Rory confessed.

"Here, have some coffee, we'll talk about it later." Jenny passed him a cup of steaming Guatemalan.

Wolfgang got up to get his coffee and walked by the stereo unit. "You guys feel like listening to some tunes?"

"Those arc dad's collection of CD's. It's either classical or jazz though."

Wolfgang sipped his coffee and leafed through CD's. "Elvis, the Sun Sessions! Rory, your dad had great taste."

"Elvis? What's that doing there? He hated Elvis."

"Maybe your dad got religion, who cares." Wolfgang put it on the CD player and pressed play. But all that came out was electronic garbage, like a modem or fax machine.

Rory walked over towards Wolfgang.

"Let's see that CD." Wolfgang, pulled out the CD and passed it to him. "That's not a CD. It's a CD-ROM."

Rory went over to where he left the bag he'd being carrying around for so long, reached in and pulled out his laptop computer. He brought it over to the kitchen table, opened it up and put the CD Rom in it.

"I thought we were looking for tapes," said Jenny.

"Maybe he transferred them. Listen ..."

Rory tapped a few commands on the keyboard and the screen came to life. Finally Victor's face came on the screen. He was silent for a moment staring out into the mini-cam or whatever he had recorded this on. Rory instinctively gulped. He hadn't seen his father for several years. Victor now looked so much older. He started to speak. Every once in awhile images of what he was talking about flashed onto the screen. He'd obviously spent some time editing the thing together.

"Rory, I never wanted to involve you in this, so I didn't tell you anything about what I am about to do. We excuse America's policies because we have been led to believe that Americans are the good guys. Well, we're not. And it's because of people like McElroy who guide our economic and foreign policies.

For years I admired McElroy and his world vision, but eventually I realized that he is a dangerous fanatic. And in audio and video recordings that I've hidden I have proof of some of his covert activities, including character assassinations of various leaders who got in the way, and of actual assassinations, including the Kennedys. McElroy leads a secret society, the Carlyle Club, of rich and powerful people who have a secret police force run by an ex-FBI agent named Hudson that looks after all the 'wet work' as they used to say. They're all ex-NSA, CIA or FBI and some still work for them.

Through these people and organizations, McElroy controls much of White House policy, but unfortunately the puppets he put in seem to believe in a Biblical Armageddon, which could lead to world war. McElroy and Thompson also have tight control of Congress and the Senate by financially owning a few key people, including the president. Almost all of whom worked for McElroy at one time or another, and have made millions off him. I realize I'm taking my life in my hands by exposing him.

McElroy's agenda is control of world governments. By taking over most of the media and much of the internet, McElroy can control information by selecting what people get. The emphasis on crime and terror in the news, for example, is to create a country in fear, making it ripe for the end of civil liberties. The war on drugs and terror have become a war on civil liberties ...

It's a new world order — in essence, to do away with democracy. They do this by economic control, and control of the World Bank and IMF. The purchase of Time Warner is one of the final pieces in their game plan. Within two years they will buy out, or put out of business most competitors and the internet will become like the monopolies the phone companies used to be.

McElroy is far richer and more powerful than any pharaoh, emperor, or king has ever been. His income surpassed the total of most countries last year. I have made copies of the video and audio tapes of meetings with some of the most powerful leaders in business and politics.

A two day conference was held at the annual Club of Brussels meetings, where this plan was finalized. I made copies. I'm meeting with Senator Joe Whitman in a few days and will pass on the originals to him. If I've been killed you must decide whether to do the same or ... destroy the copies. If you found this you'll know where the others are. I love you son."

"He's right of course," said Wolfgang, after a moment of silence. "The information revolution can kill knowledge as we knew it. Public opinion can be manipulated quicker and easier than ever before"

"But where are the tapes?" asked Jenny.

"There's only a few places here where you can store stuff. So I guess we'd better start looking," said Rory.

They spent the next couple of hours searching all the closets, cabinets and crannies, but no tapes, other than some old movies, which they dutifully checked in the old VCR.

In the end, they kind of gave up, and watched an old Hitchcock movie, North by Northwest.

Something about the fresh air had tired them out, and before Cary Grant was dive-bombed on the open range by a crazed pilot, they were all asleep.

Then, in Rory's mind the sound of the plane interrupted his sweet dream.

"... what's that sound?" he yelled. He ran to the window. "A helicopter, and it's coming this way. Get out of here!" Rory grabbed the computer, closed it and ran over and stuck it in his bag. "Let's go. Now!" he yelled at Jenny, who was frozen.

Rory grabbed her hand and pulled her towards the back door. Wolfgang, who was by now on the front balcony was about to jump over the side but his jacket got caught on the railing. He fumbled with it for a moment, tearing it loose.

A man in the helicopter with a sub-machine gun started firing at the cottage spraying the entire balcony, shattering all the windows, and hitting Wolfgang, who fell off the railing onto the verandah.

Henning appeared on the helicopter with a flame-thrower. With one burst the whole balcony went up in flames.

The television news was on. The announcer, Bob Richards, who worked with Rory for several years looked at the camera. His face looked gloomy, and he tried to put a tone of sorrow into his voice.

"A tragedy on Gambier Island, just north of Vancouver. A former member of CATV — Rory Jesson — wanted in connection with the murder of reporter, Suzanne Wilson, and apparently mentally unstable since the death of his father, went on a violent rampage, killed his two companions, and then died in a fire at his summer cottage. Here's Marie with that story..."

Rory's voice: "Tomorrow, Jenny and I are going to Fiji, and try and forget about all this. We still have a paranoid feeling McElroy's people may be after us. I've decided to abandon the search for the tapes ..."

McElroy stopped the tape recorder and looked up.

"You're sure there are no copies?"

"We took everything. His laptop. Everything, sir. The tapes are toast. Rory and the girl were both shot, escaping." said Hudson.

"It's too bad, Rory was such a nice little kid. He used to play with my son Conrad Junior, did you know that?"

"No I didn't." Hudson stood expressionless in front of McElroy who sat behind a large teak desk.

"Well how would you?"

Hudson turned to leave the office.

"Hudson, one more thing. See to it that any senator trying to stop this merger is cut off campaign funds."

"Yes sir." Hudson gave a nod, turned and left the room.

McElroy remained staring out the window, deep in thought. Suddenly the image of Victor appeared. He looked so much younger. Behind him Rory was smiling. It reminded him of the last time they had met at Victor's funeral. Rory came forward to shake his hand, but when McElroy reached for the hand, it had lunged at his throat. It remained there and started to strangle him. He gasped for air, tried to reach for his bottle of heart pills, but he couldn't move. Instead he was shaking in his chair.

After a minute the shaking stopped. The room was silent.

Epilogue

Rory woke exhausted, as if he had crammed two years into a period of a fortnight. He had been groaning and Jenny was by his side, her big brown eyes shining into his.

"Where am I?" he asked looking around the strange surroundings.

"You're at your father's cottage. We took you here to recover. You've been through an awful lot, honey."

Honey? he thought. But then it all came back, his paranoia; wandering around Vancouver like a lost puppy; Jenny and Wolf.

"Where's Wolf," Rory asked.

"Oh out and about. I think he's decided we're going to become pot growers here on this beautiful island."

"Pot growers?" But after all he had been through pot growing sounded like a normal thing to do.

"You want some breakfast?" Jenny asked, sitting up smiling.

"I'm starved, " he said. He looked around the room and started to recognize it. He could see the living room through the open door. It all looked terribly familiar.

"Hey, this is my parent's cottage."

"Now we're getting somewhere," Jenny said as she skipped out of the room laughing.